Helena and the Snow

Adam Carter

Where the page ends and life begins.

CONTENTS

ACKNOWLEDGMENTS

Thanks goes to family and friends.

1 INHERITANCE

My phone begins to ring in my bag. I let it ring, then pick it up.

"Hello, Helena speaking."

"Hi, I'm just confirming you are still meeting at the cathedral?"

"Yes, that's all the letter read, could you please tell me…" They hung up, how rude, so I put on my headphones and listen to music.

I unfold the paper under my arm. The main title reads: Immanuel Orban dies. Orban that's my surname I put two and two together he must be my relative that left me the inheritance.

I read on. A notorious hitman that the police have been trying to find dies after a fierce gun battle leaving many police officers dead. I can't read anymore, I don't want to know how it happened. I'm thankful that the train arrives at the station.

I step onto the already busy train platform. A whistle goes off in the distance as a train departs.

"Helena." I hear behind me. But I have my headphones on and pretend I didn't hear, as I have no idea who it could be and I carry on walking.

Until the hand touches my shoulder and I'm forced to remove my headphones and act interested, once my headphones are off my ears are exposed to the busy noise of people talking to one another and the screeching of the train tracks as the train pulls away.

I wipe my sweaty palms on the hem of my dress and turn around forcing a smile upon my face.

"It's me," A woman in front of me says after an awkward silence, my eyes go to her brunette hair after I don't recognise her face but it does not make me understand who she is, but I recognise those high cheekbones.

"Oh hi," My brain freezes and my brow scrunches in concentration, who is she, then it clicks. "Roxy so sorry I didn't recognize you, with your new hair."

"Yeah, well," She says blushing. "The time for crazy hair colours are gone, with me being a solicitor now." Saying the last part with a sigh, but also in triumph and tucking a piece of hair behind her ear, some confusion does she enjoy her job or not?

"A solicitor," I say she can sense in my voice that I am happy for her. "Are you heading to the office now?" I say looking her up and down in her black skirt with her shirt tucked in and her high heels, looking smart.

"Yep, I work just around the corner. Where are you off to?" She says trying to guess in her mind as I look a little too casual for work of any type.

"I am off to buy a new dress." I lie.

"So, you aren't working?"

"No, I'm in between things at the moment." I say feeling a little embarrassed, I do have money from the inheritance.

"Would you like to walk with me then. A little catch up on the way to work?"

"Sure." I say with a smile. "Lead the way."

We link arms before I am even aware of it, and we ascend the escalators to the surface, I put my ticket in the barrier machine, it eats it hungrily and the barriers open.

We meet back on the other side and take a left, down more escalators.

Luckily for me she doesn't work far so finally we stand outside.

"So," she says routing around in her bag, her tongue sticking out in concentration, pulling out a pen and piece of scrap paper. "Here is my number call me anytime, maybe we can go for a drink have a good catch up."

"Yeah, I would like that." I say with a smile and hug her, then take my leave.

I look around finding where I am. Then I remember and head for Liverpool's city centre. I grew up around here I just used to prefer online shopping, I am here for business mainly.

I received a Will from my inheritance, a key and instructions. They lay heavily on my mind as I don't know what they are for, only instructions and a location and a time eleven a.m. Checking my watch I find it's only nine.

I head to the most expensive jewellery store. I want a new bracelet. I reach the store and find a guard in a suit, ready to take out any threats to the store.

He unlocks the door and opens it for me and when I enter locks it behind me.

I look smart but there must be something about me as the women behind the counter looks at me like I won't be able to afford anything in here.

"Hi, can I help you with anything?" She asks with a smile, even her work wear oozes wealth, the blazer she wears clearly hand stitched.

"Hi. I came here looking for a bracelet. I was wondering if you could suggest anything?" I ask with a smile back.

"Can I?" She motions to my wrist with her hand, I don't know what she wants so I just offer her my arm.

She takes it and looks thinking hard. Her hands are soft, she takes out a bunch of keys and unlocks a drawer behind the counter.

"You have a nice skin complexion, I have a few here but I think this will look good on your wrist."

She hands me a solid gold bracelet with diamonds spaced evenly around, I fall in love with it instantly.

"I will take it." I say as a diamond catches in the light.

"Would you like me to package it?"

"Yes please." My voice a little too excited. Why not I think to myself.

She takes out a candle, some cloth and what looks like a stamp. She delicately cuts the cloth the right size for the box, wraps carefully, then pours a blob of red wax that seals it then stamps it with some sort of letter.

"That will be four thousand pounds."

My normal mind screams that it is too much, but I can afford such luxuries now and I haven't spent a lot of money on myself for a while. So, I take out my card and put it in the reader the woman hides her shocked face when it actually takes the money.

She hands over the package and says, "Have a nice day."

"Thanks, goodbye." I say back to her and wait at the door for the guard to unlock it, he gives me a smile as I leave.

I look at my watch again, I wasn't in their long, so I have time to go buy my gadget I wanted to originally get.

The gadget store is filled with people compared to the jewellery store, I feel the eyes on me. I feel like my dress is to short or my heels too high.

But I see the item I want a quadcopter that has a camera recording at high definition quality, it says high definition quality but not at what exact quality, just as I want to know an employee walks past.

"Excuse me." I say to him, he turns looking surprised that I am talking to him.

"Can I help you?" His name tag reads Jeff.

"Yes, I was wondering about this quadcopter, is the camera on it 1080p high definition?"

He picks up the box searching the back for information.

"Hmm," he says not finding it. "I'll go check for you."

He comes back a few minutes later.

"Sorry about that it is, 1080p yes."

"Thank you." I say with a smile and take it off him and take it to the cashier.

The register reads two hundred which isn't much considering what I just bought, even this person behind the till seems confused at me just like the women in the other shop, do I fit in anywhere? Online shopping is so much easier.

Once out the shop my phone in my bag begins to ring again. An unknown number but I answer it anyway.

"You are still heading to Liverpool Cathedral?" The voice says in a deep tone like on them movies where the person wants to stay anonymous.

"Yes," I say juggling my bags, so I can see my watch face, on time. "I am heading there now who is…" They hang up again before I can ask who it was.

I make my way slowly through the sea of people they strangely form lines the left going one way the right going the other, some people try to get to the other side and have to weave in and out.

I finally approach the cathedral, it's tall structure dwarfing the surrounding buildings. It's detailed arches and stone work always catch my breath.

Heading in I pick up a brochure that tells the history of the place and blend in with a crowd of tourists. Who am I meeting? The instructions only said to come here and walk around they will find you.

So, I break from the tourists and stand in the centre and look up, the ceiling is far above me, if giants were real ten or even twenty would have to stand on each other's shoulders to reach the top, even a dragon would stand comfortably in here.

The noises sound from afar when someone drops something, or a person speaks too loudly it travels around the building echoing then fading.

"Hello Helena." A voice from behind.

I turn to find a man, he looks to be in his forties but in good shape, his hair looks like he just got out of bed and his sunglasses to hide his eyes from the light that enters through the stained-glass windows.

"Hello, what is your name? And what am I doing here?"

"My name is irrelevant call me, what name do I like? ah call me Danny," he says clicking his fingers. "Now I am sure you know you are different from others, cold, not caring about others, let me guess you received inheritance, thought nothing of your dead relative and thought hey I got rich?"

He is right although I hate him for being right, so my silence answers and he carries on.

"Your family are part of a well-known hit squad a person needs killing your family gets the contract, but your uncle the last one alive except you, he wanted out. He struck a deal with a bodyguard company he does one last hit and the family are safe under his protection if they work for the company and get paid still. So, to business." He says rubbing his hands together. "With the snow on its way I have a month maybe two to train you, questions?"

I walk fast away from him, he's mad, train me to kill someone. I head for the elevator which takes me to another and then another. Finally I take several stairs and come out on top of the cathedral. I need air.

Danny followed me and stands silently next to me.

"What if I don't want to train with your what if I want to live a normal life?" A normal life makes me want to puke but what he is saying sounds dangerous, kill someone, I can't get over what he's asking. I don't think I'm okay with that.

"Then you will be hunted by the government and yourself and this company won't be able to help you." He folds his arms as if deeply interested in what I say next.

"How long do I have to decide?"

"You accepted the inheritance the government knows that the family line is still going, I would say a few days, maybe less."

"Then train me." I say as I don't really have a choice.

"I am glad you accept I will cost though, I told your uncle…"

"Wait, what, how much?"

"One million."

"I don't have that; the inheritance was only five hundred thousand and the house."

"Sell it then," he says with a smile. "I'm joking, with your family on the run they had to hide the money, the key, you have It?"

"Yes, yes." I find it deep in my bag amongst my things.

"Now go to the train station and find the locker there will be several million in a briefcase, carrying that much I will be close, but you won't see me. I will collect my money when the time is right."

"Fine but with my last bit of freedom I need to buy a few things."

He motions for me to go ahead and I turn on the spot heading for the exit, I look over my shoulder but can't find him even though I know he's there.

I head for a clothing store on the high street, I need to get out of these heels, I don't want to be carrying money in the wrong footwear.

Also, with the snow warning I need a new warmer coat.

I buy a fur lined jacket with a fur hood and some flat shoes, I find a space on a busy bench and sit taking off my heels rubbing my aching feet for several minutes then I slip on my flat shoes.

I take out my jacket and put it on as it is now chilly, I rub my face against the fur as it feels good on my skin.

With my heels secured in my bag I now head for the train station where I am not surprised at how busy it is.

I easily find the lockers with some assistance from the staff I show them the key and the official solicitor letter from the inheritance and they lead me to the locker.

The key fits and I slowly open it. Inside I find a suitcase and a smaller briefcase, seriously I say to myself as it has handcuffs attached to the briefcase.

Even though I don't want to look strange I know it's for the best, so I attach the briefcase to my wrist with the handcuffs and put the key in my pocket.

I am now juggling several bags, but I made sure to have my ticket ready for the barrier, I can feel the eyes on me as I stand on the escalators with a briefcase handcuffed to my wrist.

Everything on the train is making me paranoid feeling as though the person next to me could be here to kill me or they might be thinking of robbing me.

I take the train to Waterloo and head home which is close by and within walking distance of the beach, so I can start going on my daily jogs.

Once inside I place my bags on the couch then lock the door behind me.

I head straight up stairs and change into my pyjamas, now I am all nice and comfy, but I drop to the floor doing my daily press ups, once I stand I yawn and stretch. I still can't get over Danny and what he wants me to do.

I am far too tired now, so I climb into bed wrap the duvet around me and sleep as soon as my head hits the pillow.

2 TRAINING

I wake in the morning with the warm sun on my skin and lie there for a little while.

I don't want to get up I'm too comfy, I force myself to sit up wiping the saliva off my face and end up sitting on the edge of my bed my feet touching the carpet.

Rubbing the sleep out of my eyes I realize the floor is a mess with my clothes in a pile, I stretch and stand up and pick up my clothes placing them in the laundry basket. Then head to the bathroom, my hairs a mess so I manage to brush it before there is a knock on the door.

I look in the mirror my hair is now okay, my face is washed I have no makeup on, but I don't have time for that, I grab my dressing gown on the way down to hide my pyjamas.

I get to the front door, but no one is there then there's a nock again it's coming from the back door, I get to the back door finding it's locked, I run quickly upstairs getting my keys and run back to the door unlocking it I find Danny.

He walks passed me into the kitchen.

"Just invite yourself in then." I sigh, a little grouchy.

"Do you have my money?" He asks looking around.

"It's in one of the bags in the living room."

"You haven't counted it for me?" He asks pinching his nose.

I bring him the briefcase.

"If it's not in there I will bring the suitcase, just shout me I'm going to put clothes on." I say and put water in the kettle and turn it on for when I get back down.

I open my wardrobe, I have a lot of clothes inside, but I try on several outfits and can't find the right one in the end I settle for high wasted jeans and a sweatshirt. Then I do my makeup and head back downstairs.

I find Danny still counting.

"All there?" I ask pouring the kettle into a cup.

He puts down the stack he was counting, "Now I don't know where I was up to and will have to count that stack again." He says I can hear a little bit of anger in his voice.

"Okay sorry, want some coffee?"

"Tea please." His voice calmer as he begins to count again, he can be polite I think to myself.

I place the tea on the table next to him and sit at the breakfast table and pick up my book and begin to read.

Several hours later Danny packs the money back into the briefcase.

"Seems to be all there." He says closing the locks on the briefcase with a click.

"So, when do we start?" I ask placing my book down. Even though I don't want to be doing this.

"Tomorrow we will start with fitness, some hand to hand combat and then guns," He opens the back door and says. "See you tomorrow." Then closes the door behind him.

"Now what?" I say to myself it's still early, I find my quadcopter where I left it, I check if it's charged luckily it is.

I put it in a gym bag and head to the marina where I can get some footage of the beach, I only like to record places for my own use

Its early so there aren't many people at the beach only joggers or dog walkers, to my left is some radar looking building, rocks keep its shoreline safe.

The radar dish sits behind a long-barbed fence keeping trespasses away. There is a lake to my right, a boat filled with teenagers a woman standing at the front her voice shouting in rhythm, "Row, row, row."

I was impressed they were going quite fast.

I get the quad copter out of the bag and erect the aerial for the controller, I see my face in the centre of the controller showing me that the camera works.

I start up the four helicopter blades and it starts to hover above the floor, it sways left and right, crashes several times before I figure out how to properly control it.

It's in the air going steady I press record and manage to get some footage before the wind picks up and I'm forced to bring it down otherwise it may break.

I take my shoes off and feel the sand on my feet it's comforting, the wind in my hair something about it makes me feel more human.

I find a wall and sit and watch the world, the turbines far out at sea turning, the big container ships pass by into the busy port. Then the odd passenger ship passes by. More people come to the beach, but the tide comes in and people leave.

Watching the world makes me tired, I yawn and decide to head home.

I have sand in my hair from the wind, so I decide to take a shower.

Once into my pyjamas I turn the fire on, make myself a hot chocolate then sit in a chair near the fire and wrap myself in a blanket, I stare into the flames watching it dance until sleep takes me.

A nock on the back door wakes me, Danny I say to myself no one else would knock on the back door.

I open the door.

"Oh, I am glad you are taking this serious," He says looking me up and down. "A pyjama party." He says with a grin.

"Very funny I will be back down."

"Well hurry I don't have much time to take it slow you need to be trained way before the snow arrives."

He said fitness, so I put on my fitness clothes and a pair of running shoes.

I run down the stairs and find him in the back garden, I lock the door behind me.

"So, what are we doing?" I ask and stretch.

"Going for a run, keep up." He bolts across the grass and jumps the wall, okay he is fitter than I thought he was.

I leap over the wall to find him gone but I notice his foot prints and take a left where I see him running down the street towards the beach.

I watch him come to a road, but he doesn't look he sprints, a car beeps it's horn at him as it just misses him.

Danny is waiting on the other side motions as if to say your turn, is he crazy I think as I see a car coming, I sprint but fear gets the best of me and I retreat to the curb feeling embarrassed.

Danny turns and continues to run when I reach the other side I have to sprint a while just to catch him.

He waits for me at the barriers overlooking the beach.

"You need to master your fear you would have been able to nail that," He says still looking out to sea.

"It was pointless anyway just to save some time." I say taking deep breaths I feel a stitch starting in my side.

"You could have had pursuers you would have lost them."

"Okay that's a very good point," I say after thinking of another reason.

"Let's carry on, I know a spot up ahead where we can do some hand to hand combat."

I run behind him, but he eventually gets further and further ahead as the stitch gets worse, but I carry on I don't want to show weakness.

I can now see my breath in front of me as the temperature drops, I catch up to him as he waits for me at the lifeguard station, he isn't looking at me I guess he knows that I won't be able to keep up with him at first.

"We run just a little further to the sand dunes, we will do some combat there."

We reach the sand dunes where we are now out of sight and I could not feel the wind I knew it was still windy as the sand blows over the top.

"We don't have good footing to fight," I say.

"You will not always have good footing," he sinks his feet into the sand and raises his hands palms out stretched. "Come at me." He says with a grin.

There was no point in questioning I knew what we were here for, so I try to catch him off guard but my body slams to the floor.

I open my eyes as I closed them when I was slammed to the ground, he offers me his hand, I take it and he pulls me up.

"Don't rush blindly use your brain." He says.

"You are way heavy than me, I am a woman and you are heavier." I say to him as I have no confidence that I can get him to the ground as he has clearly done this his whole life.

"Your gender or weight does not matter what matters is you get a person to the ground quickly, you may still have a long journey ahead or more enemies to take down, you don't want to waste your energy on one person," He says then raises his arms. "Again," he shouts.

I go at him for several more times, but I am getting nowhere I still get slammed to the ground, my body aches and I have sand everywhere.

"Last try for the day." He says, and I am so annoyed at him standing there clearly looking pleased at the fact I haven't brought him down on my first day.

My hair sticks to my forehead I brush it out the way behind my ears and circle him this time, watching him, he moves with me in a circle, I see it, he puts more weight on his right leg.

I go at him he swings to put me to the floor, but I duck, I go for his left it is injured I can tell that, but I don't know where, so I hit at it three times before it gives in.

He goes to the ground with a slight sigh, I jump on top of him my forearm pinning his neck.

His face isn't happy, but it seems pleased.

"Well done, you went for an old injury gets me down quickest not every enemy will show weakness, but you deal with them the same, from now on I will just teach you different things we don't need to do this again," He says. "Can you get off me?"

I don't realise I was on top of him until he throws me like a twig to the side and gets up.

He brushes himself down, I do the same.

I feel proud that I got him to the ground. "Now what?" I ask feeling the energy back in me.

"We run back home we are done for the day."

He shoots off first, after a while running, I now start to feel my body aching as the adrenaline wears off.

I get back home but he carries on running it must be one of his paranoid things I head in as he didn't ask me to follow him.

I get inside and find a bunch of letters at the bottom of the door, I pick it up just to find a bunch of junk mail.

I find the remote and play my music, I realise what CD it is, I still don't understand why the singer puts her age on each album, but her songs are very good. I take off my shoes and take my bobble out of my hair it falls to my shoulders.

The bath I have feels good I sit in it for far too long and my skin goes weird but goes back to normal when I relax in my dressing gown.

3 STRANGE FEELINGS

I wake again to find myself where I remember sitting, in my dressing gown.

I search for my phone and find it's later than usual and he would knock on the door at any moment, then I hear it, knock, knock.

I quickly search for clothing and try on two different running tops before settling on a baby blue one, I grab my brush and shoes and run down the stairs.

I open the door to find a disappointed face.

"If you aren't going to take this serious then I am wasting my time." He says his face still in disappointment.

"Stop being dramatic and come inside," I say to him and head to the mirror to fix my hair. "It was my first day yesterday I was so tired and my body aches, muscles I never knew I had ache."

I look at him in the mirror his face a little less disappointed. "I suppose, let's go then." He says.

"I haven't put make up on."

"I don't have all day besides you look good without it anyway." He says and heads to the door.

My cheeks blush, he gives me a little more confidence, so I decide to not put any on, but my hair is still a mess, so I put a cap on and pull my pony tail out the back.

We run again he does the car thing, but I am ready this time and I manage to get across, I make stops when running only because my body aches, but he keeps pushing me to carry on.

We run for the next few days, he also shows me techniques to get people to the ground or a way to take them to the ground silently. Catching them as they fall was a big part.

He gives me the weekend off as a reward for being a quick learner, one of the best he has taught apparently, but I think he's just being nice.

I sleep in most of Saturday, when I wake I shower, finding bruises all over my body, one on my breast somehow.

I can't wait for training next week he is taking me somewhere to train with guns, he keeps warning me they are very illegal, but I'm not stupid.

I read my books and listen to my music, after I fix my hair, I need my rest for today.

Sunday, I wake feeling more energetic, my body aches less.

I put on my dressing gown for warmth and head downstairs, I open the fridge to find it bare, the thing is bigger than me from the previous owners, very expensive.

I suppose I have to go shopping it takes me an hour to get ready, it's freezing outside so I put on a pair of jeans, a jumper and my new jacket.

I find the suitcase with money in and take a bundle and stash it in my pocket and hide the case under my bed.

The shop is around the corner I will only need a few bits as it is for myself after all. My hand goes straight into my pocket as soon as I get outside finding my gloves.

My hands warm up almost instantly, like they were happy to get away from the cold.

Now I think maybe there will be a big snowstorm like they say, as the weather has changed dramatically, I was wearing a dress only a few days ago.

I throw myself through the door of the shop trying to act naturally but it's warmer in here. 'Ding' the doorbell goes off as I enter.

I pick up a basket and stash my gloves in my pocket. I buy the essentials and of course some chocolate for tonight when I am curled up on the chair in front of the fire.

Reaching the cashier, I find him asleep.

"Erm, hello." I say, and he still doesn't respond.

How awkward now what, poke him? Bang pans in front of his face?

I cough into my hand, clearing my throat, "Hello." I say louder.

"Err, so sorry," he says finally waking and begins to beep my shopping through each item showing on his machine. "That all?" He asks as he scans the last item.

"Yea…" I stop the newspaper catches my eye and I place it on the counter.

I give him the cash his eyes seem to sharpen up when he catches sight of the bundle of money. As I notice I quickly stash the money in my pocket. I have strange feelings about him.

"Five pence for a bag as well." He says with a smile but one of them annoying smiles.

I look in my purse and find five pence and hand it to him.

"Thanks." I say to him with a slight smile as his smile was not friendly.

The door dings behind me, I am further away from the shop when I hear the ding again, there was no one else in the shop and I could see no one on the street when I came out.

Maybe I slammed the door behind me.

Spotting a fish and chip shop on the corner I pick up pace and head straight for it, I'm cold, and it will warm me up.

Once inside the warmth again hits me.

"Hello." A man says to me from behind the counter as he tends to the food, his apron looks well used.

"Hello," I say back to him and look up at the menu behind him. "Could I get some…" I am interested as his phone goes off and he picks it up instantly.

"Yes," pause. "Yes"." Is all he says and slides the phone back into his pocket, he looks up at me that smile again on his face, he also has a scar on his forehead. "Sorry what was it you wanted?"

"I would like some chips please." I say to him now a little suspicious of him.

"Right away," he says flipping a metal thing, shakes it and places it on a wrapper and wraps it up, then places it onto of the counter. "Two pounds please." He says with his hand stretched out.

I search in my purse this time and place a two-pound coin in to his hand and take my chips and leave.

Odd people in this village.

Once home I drop my bags at the door and drop the chips on the counter and pull up a chair, they warm my belly, but I don't manage to eat them all.

I feel full and sleepy like at Christmas when you have eaten far too much, and the heating is on keeping the cold at bay and you just want to sleep.

That's what I intend to do, I kick off my shoes and get changed, climbing into bed, I roll over to find a remote, hmm is there a TV in here.

My thumb presses the power button, I hear the mechanism but unsure where from until the bottom of the bed, a blue screen appears.

The TV flickers as I flick through the flickering TV channels some of them seem to be out of tune, I find a channel that works.

The information at the bottom read: The snow, facts and lies, what's real, what's not.

An hour dedicated to the predicted snowfall in the next month or so.

Two people sat facing each other.

"So, can you tell me a fact about the snow that is said to be coming?" A young-looking TV presenter said looking over the top of her glasses for effect.

The woman on the other couch crossed her legs and placed her overlapping hands on her knees getting comfortable.

"Well it will be cold," she said with a smile. "Okay a serious fact we don't know how long it will last, we have educated guesses, a few months maybe, at max a year and then everything should be able to get back to normal."

"Will there be anywhere we can seek refuge?"

The older woman sat upright at this question.

"The government are trying their best, but we seriously don't know when the snow will hit, we can only say stay running from the snow, the North of Scotland will be hit first it will be terrible up there."

"Yes, I have heard on the news they are evacuating them immediately as they of course won't know until it's too late."

Their detailed conversation was making me fall asleep trying to keep track of the back and forth conversation made my eyes drop.

So, I pressed the power button and the mechanism kicked in again. Once the blue screen had gone I put my head on the pillow.

Yep I did it again the knocking on the door and my head begins to spin, the knock is normal at first then it gets slow and deliberate as if to say if you don't open the door there will be consequences.

I sprint down the stairs slide on my feet through the hallway and swing open the door, luckily it was Danny or that would have been embarrassing.

Once he is inside I close the door he sits down with a disappointed look and I walk slowly to the stairs, once out of sight I run up the stairs to the bedroom dressing quickly, washing quickly and putting on my jacket.

"We will be taking the train to Southport and walking for few hours to some countryside start your gun training." He says without taking his eyes off his newspaper.

What's he waiting for I think.

My eye catches his boots I slip away and change and put on walking boots and head back to the kitchen where he folds the paper and stands up.

"Let's go." He says.

He's walking fast, but I can keep up now that I am well, I would consider myself quite physically fit.

It's cold outside but maybe the big warm jacket wasn't a good idea as I start to get warm quickly.

"Might want to put on a cap," he says as we near the station, putting on his own cap.

"I don't have a…" My voice trails off as I feel something in my pocket and pull out a cap.

He grins as I know I didn't put it there.

I put the cap on and pull my pony tail out the back and follow Danny.

We walk right past the ticket machines and head to the platform.

"Aren't we paying?"

"Check your other pocket." His voice sounding bored.

No, he couldn't have snuck a cap and a ticket into my pocket without me knowing, he wasn't even that close to me to be able to.

I see the orange bars on the ticket before I pull it fully out of my pocket, return to Southport.

"Okay how did you do that?"

"You took way too long to get ready I had plenty of time your jacket was downstairs it wasn't hard." He says but keeps looking straight at well nothing.

I look at the information board, two minutes, we wait the train finally pulls up a door stops exactly where Danny is, but he doesn't move the door opens and he steps on and stands near the door.

4 INTELLIGENCE

The train journey was like any ordinary train journey quite boring except for the scenery but we don't sit down, and Danny looked on edge.

The train stops, the doors barely open before Danny jumps out, lands and walks fast.

He takes us to find a taxi.

"I thought we was walking?"

"Yes, but are you crazy? nowhere near Southport, we are taking a long journey into the countryside." He says while climbing into the front seat of the taxi.

I climb in the back but only hear the taxi driver.

"That will cost quite a bit." The taxi driver says with a yawn and scratches his ear.

Danny flashes cash and the engine starts.

"So, what you two up to in the countryside some hiking?"

"An extra fifty pound if you don't ask questions." Danny says his voice slightly annoyed.

The taxi driver looks and nods without saying anything we drive an hour maybe more, stopping at a car park the scenery has changed buildings are far and in-between.

"Here okay?" The taxi driver asks looking at Danny.

"It's fine here," He hands him a stack of cash. "Keep the change."

The car screeches off flicking dust in the air.

"So where now?" I ask kicking a stone.

"Over that hill should be a guy waiting for us."

We walk for a while; the sun starts to set causing the temperature to drop we get over the hill.

"Get on your knees, hands in the air!" A voice shouts in the distance.

Danny grabs me and slams me into a tree I can see him reach for something tucked into his belt and hear a click.

Next, it's a waiting game, I know to stay quiet I know Danny has a gun.

A twig snaps nearby, Danny moves and points his gun seconds later a torch comes on, it's the guy who was shouting who has the torch on his gun, it's pointed at Danny and his pointed at him.

"Danny, good I thought you was an unwanted visitor, follow me." His voice is deep he looked taller, but I won't know what he looks like until morning.

"Helena," He says. "Your sleeping area." The flashlight shines for a second and I see it, a small tent.

I fumble in the darkness and find a zip, once inside I zip it up again.

Now I feel stupid I have a torch in my pocket, I find the button and I can see there is a sleeping bag inside.

Taking off my boots and jacket I find it even colder, I use my jacket for a head rest and quickly climb into the sleeping bag.

Sleep found me easily after that long walk, but full rest isn't given as I get torch in my face in the morning.

"Wake up breakfast is done." It's the guy I don't know yet.

Once ready I leave the tent finding Danny bent over a fire with what looks like a rat, no most likely a rabbit.

"Hope you aren't vegetarian." He says with a smirk.

The other guy seems to be on drugs or very paranoid he keeps his gun close to him finger near the trigger constantly looking into the distant trees.

"What's your name?" I ask.

"Why you undercover police?"

"She asks a lot of questions this one." Danny says his eyes still on the food.

"You don't need my name I teach you few days how to use gun then you never see me."

"Okay when do we start?" I ask and take a piece of meat off Danny.

"Once you eat that, hurry."

His words seem fast and rushed adding to the paranoia that clearly affects him.

"Damn government probably spying on me now. They been trying to get me long enough." He says under his breath as he leads us off into the trees.

We reach a green army looking vehicle, I climb in the back and we head off onto bumpy dirt roads finally stopping at a clearing.

"Far away from anywhere a perfect spot, hand me that." He points at a bag next to my feet.

I pass it to him, it's heavy.

We walk onto the clearing where there is a table and bottles at the far end.

He reaches into the bag brings out a pistol, checks the magazine and clicks it.

"Ready to go let's see what you can do first."

I wrap my hand around the gun feeling my finger touch the trigger, aim down the sight control my hands and squeeze.

The glass smashes.

"Hmm," The man says he has binoculars. "Good for an amateur but you hit the right of the bottle if it was a person you would have hit the arm, given them a flesh wound, hold it close to your face. Wrap your other hand around it as well, try again."

I squeeze the trigger surer this time but still I can't tell so I look at him.

"Perfect are you sure you haven't done this before?"

"It's in her genes you know who her family is." Danny says waving his hand. "Now can we move onto bigger weapons?"

"I am sure shooting a gun can't be in her genes but maybe fight instead of flight may be stronger in them, I don't know maybe something mental." This guy shocks me he seemed a little stupid but now I know how he has managed to evade capture.

He pulls out a shotgun with a smirk.

First, he shows me how to load it pull the grip back to load.

I know these give a kick, we move closer to the target, I squeeze the trigger and somehow manage to stay on my feet.

But my shoulder hurts now.

"How can you manage every weapon I hand you." He says with slight annoyance in his voice.

He opens his jacket and pulls out a huge handgun, bigger than his shovel like hands.

My girly hands just manage to wrap around it when he hands me it.

"Try that." He says laughing.

The trigger squeezes and the gun slips out of my hand.

"Finally, something you can't handle."

The man scratches his stubble on his quite large chin, then pulls out a shiny new looking gun.

"These are yours," He pulls out a few holsters and some guns. "Some advice never get caught."

"Yeah, he gave me the speech, so are you also carrying a gun?" I ask turning to Danny.

Danny moves his jacket to the side showing a gun in a holster by his ribs, then let's his jacket fall back into place.

"I think anyone you meet from now on might have one a good way to start thinking always be in reach of your weapon, I chose those guns for you, try them out."

The gun feels just right in my hands not too heavy not to light, I know now how to check the clip and find it full.

A few rounds get fired down range all hitting the target I do seem to be a natural. But I still hate what he's training me for and that I have no choice.

"We will carry on tomorrow put your holsters on and make sure the damn safety is on your weapons. Oh, and here." He throws what look like round barrel like objects. "Silencers you will use them. Well at all times really unless they know you are coming."

I pocket them and awkwardly at first put the holster on but figure it out in the end it goes just under my armpit near my ribs.

The night is cold, I get warm in my sleeping bag and drift off.

I wake suddenly in the night as I hear the zip of the tent being undone. I instantly reach for the gun and hold it with two hands.

"Freeze." I say calmly which surprises myself.

I hear laughter and then see his face in the moonlight it's the man that I do not yet know the name of.

"Freeze like the movies, it was a test you passed you don't want people sneaking up on you."

He leaves and zips the tent back up, I struggle to get the gun back into the holster even though I managed to get it out easily, I blame it on the adrenaline making my fingers clumsy.

"Get up, quickly we are leaving."

It's Danny's voice I quickly get up pull on my boots and head outside.

Danny just points in the direction and we both start to run, we come to the man's car and jump inside.

"What's going on?" I ask.

"Police helicopter I think they have intelligence."

We drive fast for a moment I think we are going to crash as he steers it towards a rock wall, but we end up in a cave, quickly the engine goes off and we plunge into silence.

We wait for what seemed like hours, when we drive out a soft snowfall begins.

"Good," The man seems to announce. "Snow storm will keep em away, I will drop you two off in the village."

"So, we are finished with my training?" I ask feeling a little worried.

"Yes, you seem like a natural anyway."

He swerves to miss a tree, I nearly fall into the middle seat, my own fault for not wearing a seat belt.

"It's just over here, both of you get ready to get out."

We get over the hill, but the two front wheels only manage to make it on the road before something slams into us.

The last thing I see is the car tumbling, I feel like a doll in a washing machine until I finally pass out.

I wake to the sound of gun fire thudding into the cars metal, I can hear a quieter gun fire return.

My head aches, a lot of my body is in pain most likely bruising as I can still move without being in total agony.

I feel around to find I am on the roof of the car, yet again I realize my own stupidity of no seat belt.

I right myself and climb out the shattered window trying to avoid the broken pieces of glass.

I stagger and go to stand but get my head pushed back down, I look up finding it was Danny, he continues to squeeze the trigger.

"Pass me that." He shouts.

I grab the clip and pass it to him.

"Well are you going to help?"

Oh yeah, I pat under my arm both sides finding the guns still in the holsters, I pull one out and stand next to Danny and take aim.

It's the first time I see the situation, two black vans all doors open, block the road.

They look like police, but they don't wear any badges. I see one pop his head out from behind the van, I squeeze the trigger, it hits close as he hides back behind the van.

Another takes aim on the bonnet, I see the flash of the gun, the bullet flies past me, flicking my hair as it does.

I take aim myself and manage to hit him in the shoulder.

"Cover me." Danny says and seems to climb back into the car.

One of them notices his absence and tries to advance.

I fire hitting him in the chest, he goes down but doesn't move, I killed him why don't I feel anything.

I should feel sad at least but I don't, why don't I.

I snap back as something is thrust into my knees.

"Grab that."

I grab the bag and throw it over my shoulder.

"Let's go." He takes one last look over his shoulder then grabs my arm and leads me into the woods towards the village.

5 BRUISES AND BLOOD

"Who were they?" He doesn't answer. "Were they after me?"

"No, the ones after you are more ruthless, they were after him."

"Were they police?"

"Sort of," he says stepping over a fallen tree. "They are trained enough that if it went wrong they just class it as a gang attack."

"More ruthless but they haven't caught me yet."

There was silence walking through the forest it's so peaceful, the different shades of green, but why aren't my thoughts on the man I just killed, maybe he is right I am made for this, but I still don't want to be doing this.

We finally see a building up ahead through the trees, must be the village, but I can't think properly as my head still aches.

I push my way through the hedges and bump into Danny who seems frozen.

I look around and notice we're in someone's garden, a woman is putting washing on a line, she stops holding clothing mid-air.

"You two look like you need a cup of tea." She said in a soft voice and continued to put washing on the line.

"I could do with something stronger." Danny says and laughs, the woman does too.

"Come." She says and turns walking inside.

Once I am inside I notice no pictures on the walls, no family or friends.

"So, what brings you here?" I watch her pick up the TV remote and switch it on.

A banner at the bottom repeats: breaking news.

"Breaking news," A news reporter says shuffling his papers. "Reports of gun fire on the streets between a gang and rivals yet to be confirmed by the police." He touches his ear as his face focuses. "Reports on the ground confirm one of the gang members died in the firefight, a man and women still out there armed and dangerous."

The women turns to us looking more at Danny.

"Don't say anything." She says before Danny could speak. "I will drop you off where you want but then I'm calling the police."

"Why are you so calm?" I ask feeling a little dizzy still from the crash.

"You don't look like the gang warfare type to me, I assume you are in something, you don't look like the mass murder type of girl to me, if it was him on his own I would have said I was making tea and called the police right away."

She picks up her keys from a table and leads us to a door where she slips some shoes on and grabs a coat.

Danny and I climb in the back it's a small car and my knees touch the seat in front of me.

Once out the road we head south towards Southport.

"Where do you want me to drop you off?" She says looking in the rearview mirror.

"Just outside Southport if you can please." Danny says and stretches his head to look out the back.

"Police." I shout as I see the blue flashing light up ahead.

"Damn it," The woman says. "Pretend to be lovers or something sit closer together they don't have your description yet."

Danny moves into the seat that's between us and puts his arm around me, this feels alien, but I know it must be done so I lean into him.

We get closer, it's a checkpoint, the woman stops, and he asks for her driver's license she hands it over.

"Who are those two in the back?" He asks.

"That's my brother Tony and his girlfriend Alexandra."

He seems to stare at us and nods I feel relieved. "Okay carry on then." He says and hands her driver's license back.

We drive off slowly, I hear a click and find Danny had his hand in his jacket his gun pointed at the window, once around the corner the woman drives faster.

"Stop up here please." Danny says as we reach the high street.

We get out and quickly walk through the busy street, once at the train station we hear sirens in the distance.

Danny stops and grabs my arm pulling me around a corner.

"What?" I ask rubbing my arm as his fingers dug into my skin.

"Police in the station. Are your guns secure?"

I pat them and nod my head.

He grabs my hand and interlocks his fingers and pulls me close. We show our tickets to the guard and slowly walk past the police officer.

My heart slows down once we get past him and jump on the train, my breathing starts to calm down.

Danny doesn't look any different like we were not almost caught by a police officer and sent straight to jail.

"Our training is done. I will pick you up at six on Saturday put your finest clothes on."

"Where are we going?"

"To see the target, you will have the week to look at the files. Then you will take care of him and the snow will hit the rest of your life is up to you once the snow goes."

His words tick in my mind, you will take care of him.

"Aren't you getting off?"

I look around and realize we are at Waterloo I jump off in time as the train doors beep and close.

Danny stays on and I head home slowly like I have so much weight on my shoulders. I am being hunted and my only way out is to kill someone.

Once home I decide to lay in bed with hot chocolate and see what's on TV the snow begins to fall on and off through the night.

I keep up my running during the week but decide not to on Wednesday I didn't even realize what day it was until I found a calendar.

Again, I stay in bed nice and warm and comfy in my pyjamas, I have been having far too many lazy days.

I hear a handle being tried downstairs then a window smashes, I freeze and grab tightly to my quilt pulling it over my chest and hug it.

Then I hear the voices.

"I followed her here she should be running, she does it every morning, so we have to be quick search for anything that pins her to the Orban family."

"We are told it is her we should not be in here. We should have bagged and tagged her."

There seems to be only two, but I am frozen in place. Get up I say to myself several times and manage to get out the bed at least and tip toe to my guns lying on the chair.

I pick up one and attach the silencer.

"The bins full she is staying here."

I hear their boots moving around the room downstairs.

I don't have time to put shoes on, so I tip toe barefoot down the stairs with my back to the wall.

I stop and listen one is in the kitchen, but I have no idea where the other is as I can't hear his boots. I lean and spot one in the kitchen he turns and spots me.

He does two things, goes to pull his gun and shout. I squeeze the trigger send two bullets in his chest. My foot touches the cold laminate flooring and I head to the kitchen, slowly, quietly.

I know the other one is here, and he heard the body hit the floor.

I see a shadow to my left and try to turn my gun, but he smacks it out of my hand it drops and slides into the kitchen.

I drop to the floor as his weight hits into me.

He laughs. "An Orban family member the last one and you were sleeping in your pink pyjamas pathetic." He laughs again. "You will die in your pyjamas." He's already annoying me.

"At least I will die comfy." His smirk fades.

He goes to pull his gun I look to my left and find a pile of hardback books and grab it. I throw it at him when he goes to look where his gun is. It hits him right in the forehead.

I stand up quickly and get a blow to his ribs before he realizes I am standing.

I dodge his first punch and catch him in jaw with my fist, he staggers backwards but continues to come at me.

He throws two punches I dodge the first but the second gets me in the ribs it hurts badly I go to my knees, he tries to kick me, but I grab his leg and pull.

He lands on the floor with a thud, I turn and try to scramble on the floor for my gun but feel a hand grab my ankle I try to kick but he pulls, grabs me and tosses me into the wall.

A sharp pain shoots through my back, I use the table I am next to, to get up and find a vase I get my hand around it by the time he grabs my shoulder and turns me around.

I duck his most liked punch to the face and bring the vase up and smash it into his face glass flies everywhere some goes in my hand but his right side of his face bleeds, pieces of glass sticking out.

He shouts in pain, I punch him in the ribs, but he manages to get me off guard and gets me in the face.

I find an ornament it's heavy, I put all my weight behind it and ram it into his head he drops to the floor unconscious or dead I don't check.

I drop to the floor in relief it hurts again to move, there is a piece of glass in my hand, but the fight took all my energy.

I'm going to take a bath I don't even care anymore. I get my gun first then struggle getting up the stairs and my pink pyjamas are ruined with all the blood.

There are blood droplets leading right to the bathroom door meaning if there is more I'll be leading them right to me, but I couldn't care less anymore, I lock the bathroom door behind me

I strip out of my dirty pyjamas and slowly walk to the cabinet and pull out a first aid kit. The glass hurts like nothing I felt before as I slowly pull it out.

My hand is a mess, but I clean and bandage it before I lose any more blood, the sink is a mess but again I couldn't care anymore I need a bath I sit with no clothes waiting for the bath to fill and then lower myself into it.

I put the gun on the ledge next to me and relax as much as I can, trying not to focus on the two dead bodies downstairs and the back door wide open.

I hear a door downstairs being kicked in. Oh, please just leave me alone, leave my doors be.

They get in and their boots go quiet as they must have stumbled upon the first body or even seen the second in the kitchen.

Then I hear the stairs creaking they are following the blood droplets, ugh why just why, I pick the gun up and fire at the door, wood flies in the air and the creaking stops.

"Helena, it's me Danny."

I place the gun back on the ledge.

"Good."

"Are you okay?"

"I've felt better."

"Can you open the door?"

"I am naked, so no."

"Sorry. I didn't know sorry." The only time I hear Danny's voice not calm.

"Can you sort the doors out at least?"

"I have a team coming."

"Then get me a towel please and some clothes out of my wardrobe."

The hot water soothes some of my pain but when I go to climb out the pain hits me in my ribs and back.

"I have your clothes." Danny says.

I use all my strength to get out the bath and unlock the door. I open it wide and hide behind the door.

"Don't come in," I quickly say. "Just throw them in make sure you miss the blood."

He launches the clothes in, they land on the window ledge, I slam the door then quickly run to stop them falling in the sink. Then lock the door.

6 TARGET

It takes me a while to get dressed as I only have one fully working hand, it's snowing outside, and he decided to give me shorts and a t-shirt.

The team still hasn't arrived when I unlock the door, so the house is freezing, and I can feel it on my legs.

"What made you decide shorts was the best option to get?" My voice sounds weak. I shake off the cold.

"Sorry I wasn't thinking fashion." I laugh, and he follows behind me into the bedroom.

"Throw some logs on the fire and close the door please."

I sit on the warm arm chair and put my knees to my chest. "Pass me my blanket."

He puts it on me and starts the fire.

He sits on the arm chair opposite and laughs.

"What are you laughing at?" I say and yawn.

"You had to do it in Orban style."

"What do you mean?"

"You killed two people I find blood everywhere and you are relaxing in a bath. Your uncle killed two people in a bar once, there was two more on the one contract, so he sat at the bar and drank a few drinks until the other half of the contract walks in he kills them finishes his drink and leaves."

I laugh it is quite funny now I think of it except for the pain part.

"I knew them two now that I think of their faces. One was from the chip shop down the road the other from the grocery store."

"Good they are from the ruthless group coming after you, they won't come into your house again after losing two of their operatives."

In the morning I wake up and move finding my muscles also in pain. Danny is nowhere to be seen.

I put on a dressing gown and some jogging pants as the chill in the house brushes against my arms and legs.

The blood in the bathroom has been cleaned but the door hasn't been renewed but the downstairs door has, and the bodies and other debris have been removed.

I spend the rest of the week upstairs, downstairs just feels strange I only go down there to make food and bring it up and eat in bed watching TV.

It's now Saturday Danny will be here at six, so it will take me most the day to get ready, wash my hair, nails, shoes, too much effort but I guess we are going somewhere fancy, so I put in the effort.

I am ready by five but struggle to choose a dress and settle with a red one that matches my nails and black heels.

A bruise on my arm still hasn't healed so I hide it with makeup.

I put a gun in my purse as I don't trust anyone now and I can't put it anywhere else.

Danny knocks on the door exactly at six.

"Wait in there." I say and run up the stairs to get my things.

I get back down the stairs and see him properly, he is wearing a suit looking smart.

"You look beautiful." He says to me.

"Thanks, let's go." I quickly say before I start blushing. I put on my long coat that stops below the knee.

The door now locked I turn and find Danny holding the door open to a limousine. I climb inside it has champagne waiting, I take a sip, but I'm not a fan.

"Where are we going?"

"The city centre to an expensive restaurant. This will be the last time we meet."

"Why?"

"I have done all I can to get you ready. I cannot force you to pull the trigger but if you want a normal life you will. The target will also be there."

"Why don't I just kill him there then?"

"Because you will be caught and charged, you will do it while he is on his boat just off the marina near where you live. It will all be in the file."

Silence fills the limousine until it pulls to a halt and the door is opened for me by the driver.

"Thank you." I say to him and he bows.

The double doors are opened for us as we reach them. Inside, the roof is high, and both the roof and walls are gold, real gold or not I have no idea, but I am impressed.

A man with a curled moustache greets us. "Welcome, do you have a reservation?"

"Yes." Danny says and pauses like he is remembering. "Smith, I think the person on the phone said we are the third Smith reservation."

The guy searches a list. "Ah here, yes a lot of Smiths today very popular. Table four, may I take your coats."

We hand him our jackets Danny takes out a leather folder, the employee hangs them up and says, "Follow me this way."

He takes us to a table for two in the centre next to everyone else.

"How's the hand?" I quickly take it off the table and rest it on my knee.

"It's getting better no infection at least. So where is the target?"

"Over there behind you, in the booth." I go to turn my head, but I'm stopped by the shock when I feel Danny's hand on mine. "Don't look." He says as I turn my head to look at him.

"Why?" I ask and move my hand away from his.

"Because that will make it obvious you are looking at him, look at his guards all around the room they are watching everyone."

I take my bag off the table. "Where is the bathroom?"

The corner of his lips turns up as he knows. "Around the booth."

I stand clutch my bag and walk as soon as I turn I notice him, two women with him both laughing and clinging to each arm. His hair is jet black gelled into a spike.

Everyone else is wearing smart wear but he wears jeans and a t-shirt. I want to take my gun out and wipe that smug look on his face as he winks at me when I pass.

A guard stands behind the booth and opens the bathroom door for me.

"Thank you."

I don't even need to be in here, but it will look suspicious if I leave now so I carefully unwrap the bandage to have a look and clean it then put new bandages on.

The guard is still standing there when I leave but the target as Danny puts it, is nowhere to be seen. There is a plate and glass of wine where I am sitting.

"I ordered for you hope you don't mind, I read in your file from when you were a child that you liked lasagne." He takes a sip of his own wine. "The wine I had to guess."

"My files from foster care maybe once I am done here I will go and find my files and burn them."

"No need already did that once I read them of course." He takes a mouthful of some odd-looking food.

I pick up my knife and fork and cut into my food, the hot steam escapes. I take a bite and it is really nice best one I have ever tasted.

"Why did you burn it?"

He sips his wine. "It contains your weaknesses not much was there, but I still burnt it anyway."

He knows, I am interested in what he read but he just sits there eating away. I finish mine first and look around the room, everyone in their finest clothes, their clothes and looks ooze money.

"What did you find out about me in my files then?" I finally ask.

"Just like I expected, struggles to connect with people, doesn't obey authority." He didn't find the psychiatrist report. "I found other ones that where online." He found them. "A psychiatrist report very, very interesting that's why I agreed to your uncle to take on the contract of helping you."

"Oh."

"Oh." He says I am staring at the table that report was personal he shouldn't have looked. "Besides a few illnesses he said you were a different child very caring but disconnected like you loved the world but at the same time hated the rules of society and how everything interacts. I was so fascinated."

"We both know there was a lot more in that report." I say and take the glass and finish off my wine.

"Yes, but that's old news I got rid of all traces. You can join the army or foster a child if you wanted. Hey even adopt." He smiles knowing I wouldn't like any of that.

"What's in the file?" He has had his hand on it the whole time.

"Your assignment all the details are in there, there's no need for me to tell you in a room full of guards, take it home read it fully the date is in there when you will do it." He stops a waiter walking by. "I would like to pay."

"Certainly sir."

He comes back with a check and lays it on the table.

He writes a check and hands it back. "There's an extra two hundred there for whatever she wants, bring her a bottle of wine." The waiter nods and leaves to get it. "I am leaving now the limousine will be waiting outside, it will take you home. This is goodbye and good luck."

He kisses me on the head and leaves. I didn't have the chance to say thanks or what if my house gets broken into again, but he is gone now it's all up to me, well and the information in the folder but I will look at that tomorrow.

I drink half the bottle and leave myself, there's a different guy behind the counter I tell him which coat is mine and he helps me put it on.

I wait on the pavement looking for the limousine it pulls up and I ride alone home, my heels are killing my feet, so they come off immediately, it's raining when we reach home, so I run barefoot tip toeing to the door and quickly unlock it.

I am again too tired to change so I drop onto the bed and let sleep take me.

When I wake I have to think where I am, ha I slept in the spare bedroom I didn't even notice where I was last night probably too much wine.

I have only been in here once it's a nice bedroom not as big as the master bedroom. It's still big a double bed, wardrobe. dressing table and a writing desk.

The door closes spookily behind me before I head down the stairs I notice the bullet hole still in the bathroom door I should get it fixed but I have bigger things on my mind.

My foot hovers over the first step of the stairs when I realize I am still wearing my dress, okay maybe the alcohol hasn't fully worn off.

It takes me a while, but I finally settle on a pair of jeans and a tank top, but a light snow has started so I feel a little cold and put a white fur blanket around my shoulders.

My heels are on the floor in the hall, but I have no idea where my jacket is but it's my jacket for going out somewhere nice I will find it by then, but the file where did I put it.

7 DEATH

It took me a few hours to find the file but eventually I found it in the bedroom, so my drunk mind put it in the master bedroom then wandered into the spare bedroom and slept. Maybe I should not drink for a while.

Once I have poured my hot chocolate and poked the fire I sit in the living room with the black folder laying on the table.

The first page is the guy I saw in the restaurant. His name underneath reads: Unknown. Yeah right basically they don't want me to know his name because it's isn't important.

It would, to be fair, make me search him up on the Internet. For all I know this could all be a set up, but I have no choice, or my house will never be a safe place or even I will never be safe.

The next page is his whereabouts on a boat off the marina, the next few pages are his charges. Multiple accounts of, well everything, drugs, guns, human trafficking. He even supposedly had a whole village killed because they tried to steal from him.

I read on and everything inside me really wants him dead now, but I have been told to wait until the next weekend. I find instructions at the back, kill him use his phone to call the police and then head straight home, pack winter clothing then leave for the North as soon as the snow hits work your way south to Cornwall.

Once the snow clears head home where everything should be fine. They used the word should be, sounds promising. Sounds nice and simple when they put it in instruction form.

I start running again but I am faced with a question run with a gun or not. I choose to run with a gun but find several issues, running clothing is tight I can't run with it flashing about, so I run wearing a light weight waterproof jacket to hide it.

Once I run to the beach I do several push ups before running home, once home I get to chill and read but the constant reminder I must attack a yacht in a few days' time lies heavily on my mind.

Each day I run it feels like I am running closer to that day. He isn't a good man, but will I be able to take a life.

I run faster and further each day trying to drain my own thoughts out. I can't even read as my mind is elsewhere.

Saturday morning the day has come. Tonight, I will have to assault a yacht in a boat that should be waiting for me with strict instructions to use the paddles once close so not to alert any alarms, that'll be fun. Not.

None of it will be fun but it seems like all of it will be necessary to try and get myself away from the hit squad on the Orban name.

I wash my hair and tie it in a pony tail, so it won't go in my eyes. I wear black suit pants, a shirt and a blazer with the two-gun holsters under my arms and smart flat shoes.

I look in the mirror I have to look good in case I end up dead. My heart races as the sun starts to go down I can't keep still and pace the bedroom.

It's time, I grab my long length coat but don't button it up, so I can get to my guns and head out.

The snows still falling but only lightly and the rain washes most of it away. The marina is almost pitch black when I reach it. As it has no lights at all.

I head over the rocks onto the beach where I find a boat waiting for me. I grab hold of the lever and pull and pull again until the engine roars into life.

It's loud so I know why they want me to row when I get close. I can see the yacht on my right, it's lights illuminating it and it isn't moving so I know that's it.

The waters a little choppy and snow continues off and on I get close and kill the engines and fumble around on the boat. Touching wood, I find the two oars.

I put them into the water and begin to row the boat goes slow at first. Sometimes my efforts are pointless as a wave just pushes me back, but I reach the yacht, there's no movement on deck.

At first, I think I have to swim but they have a lower deck where two jet skies are attached.

The boat taps the yacht gently as a wave pushes it. There's a piece of spare rope so I attach it to my boat, well their boat whoever it belongs to.

I hear footsteps above me I quickly stick to the wall. A shadow is cast down upon the deck I am on. So, whoever it is must be at the railings above me.

I slowly reach inside my coat and pull out my gun and attach a silencer. There's stairs upwards to my left, quietly I tip toe upwards.

I don't hear anyone move so I quickly go up the last few steps turn and fire. The body falls over the railings with a loud thud hitting the deck below.

It was a guard I seen his black basic uniform and gun on his hip. So, I know I am on the right boat but where is the target.

There's a door behind me. The target must be in the sleeping quarters. I open the door a largish room where they would entertain guests.

I hear again footsteps, I run to the wall I glimpse a black shirt coming from stairs down the corridor.

"The boss wants champagne." I hear a guard say. He's close.

Peeking around the corner he is just there within reaching distance. I go to take him out with my hands, but he turns around. Both of us get a fright and punch blindly I'm sent in the air back into the room.

I grab a lamp and throw it as he reaches for his gun. Mine is on the floor but I get my second one in time as he runs at me. I pull the trigger and his body goes limp and lands on me.

I use all my strength and roll him off me. A chef stands in the doorway.

I raise my weapon.

"Please don't," he says his hands in the air. "I won't say anything I am just the chef."

I flick my wrist motioning for him to leave, he does. My ribs hurt after that punch, but I carry on. The kitchen is clear now just downstairs where he must be.

Tip toeing again but I don't know if the element of surprise is lost. No one has come up the stairs, so I guess not.

My shoe slips off as I quickly yank my foot back up the stairs as a bullet just misses it.

"You lose a shoe?" I hear from around the corner.

"No, I have a spare." I hear a laugh, but he knows his job and I know mine.

He is to the left, retrace my steps or suppress him then try to get a clean shot.

He isn't that good of an aim if he missed my foot, but my feet are small. He fires again and puts a bullet in my shoe just to let me know he is still there.

Okay so maybe he is a better shot than I thought. I am going to risk it. I jump. I feel my body fly through the air, my head slams into the wall.

I don't even see as pain jolts through my spine. But I squeeze the trigger several times until one of my guns clicks signalling no ammo.

He pops his head out of a door and gets a shot it rips my pants, blood surfaces, but it didn't enter. I wait as he quickly went behind his cover.

As soon as his head pops out I get him, and he falls into the corridor.

I take a further look at the wound it's quite deep, but I can fix it myself later. I pick up my shoe my toes would stick out the end if I put it on, so I take off my other shoe and put them both in my pocket.

I am now shoe less and bleeding and that jump hurt more than I thought it would. The door at the end, double doors I guess he is in there.

Four guards run out of a door I manage to drop two before the other two reach me. No guns I guess they were sleeping, heavy sleeping to miss all what's gone on.

Luckily only one can come at me at a time. He punches my thigh where the bullet caught me. I scream in pain but use the pain as anger and punch him in the face with all my force his noes pops and blood pours out.

He falls back and lets the next man come at me. He grins and goes into a stance he seems more aware. I throw a punch, but he tosses my hand away. It's like this is a game to him.

I throw a punch but pull back and try to kick him instead. He grabs my leg bad mistake as his pulls my leg and I end up on the floor. He is on me before I can get up.

His legs pin mine and his arms pin mine.

"What the boss will do with you." He smirks.

His leg slips as I wiggle trying to get free I bring my knee and it connects with his groin. I use my legs and arms and throw him over my head.

Another bad mistake now they both can come at me at the same time.

And that's what they do. I look between them both, I am trapped. But I run up the wall and turn, my hand connects with his face which then connects with the wall knocking him out. Now the one with the popped noes faces me.

My toes touch metal I glance it's my gun. He also looks at my gun, he jumps in the air like a tiger I drop to the floor and fire. His body slams into me and pins me against the wall.

I walk over the bodies, so much death all because of one man. Now I have both my guns in hand. I head straight for the doors there's no knowing what's on the other side.

I raise the weapons in front of me and kick the door.

He is lying on the bed with a girl a guard aims his weapon we both fire his hits my arm I look another deep flesh wound.

But my aim is true, and he drops to the ground. I don't let the man speak it will just alter my judgement, so I kill him where he lies. The woman isn't my target, so I leave her screaming behind me and close the door.

I make sure I haven't left anything behind my shoes are in my pocket, only my blood but I am sure that will get taken care of.

The ship decks cold as it's snowed slightly heavy. My thoughts are empty trying not to think what's just happened. The realization hits me when I am on the boat and I need space I can't breathe.

Close to the shore I jump into the water and run for the beach I reach it and lie on the sand breathing heavy, my chest rises and falls I eventually manage to get my breathing under control.

The snows falling around me, but I can't move not yet. As I get my breathing under control the adrenaline rush leaves and my flesh wounds sting as the salt water has gotten inside.

I stumble home lucky it's close as my feet start to get really cold and so does my body as the swimming was a bad idea.

I get home and find an alcohol bottle and pour into my wounds. I find bandages and wrap it tightly around now I look at the alcohol bottle and take a long drink without stopping until I pass out.

8 FLEEING

I hear a smash and quickly wake only to find it was the bottle had rolled out of my hand. Today I must leave my house even if I am still in pain.

There is dirt on my feet and then I remember the long walk home. First thing I do is shower then go into my room and get a bag.

But what to pack? The snow is off and on and who knows how long before I can come back here. I throw in underwear, an extra sweat shirt and an extra pair of jeans.

I literally just threw them in so now I have to fold them, ugh annoying. I change myself into several outfits before finally settling for jeans and a light pink sweatshirt and my walking boots.

What else do I need, I look around the room and put on my bracelet I have become attached to. Of course, I grab my new warm jacket with a fur hood.

What else ah some money, where I left it in a cupboard in the kitchen I grab a few stacks and line my pockets then hide some under my clothes in the bag.

I am not leaving the rest of the money easily to be found so I go back to the bedroom peel up the carpet and pull back a floorboard and shove it under there.

I may need my guns, so I attach my holsters before putting on my jacket grabbing my bag and then take one last look before heading out the door and locking it. I feel like I'm fleeing.

The snow falls on my hair and it's freezing, I like snow, but every day is kind of annoying. I walk down the road before calling a taxi it arrives a while later.

"Taxi for Helena?" A guy asks when I open the door.

"Yes, but I was wondering do you do long journeys?"

"Depends where to?"

"Lake District, Windermere?"

"Windermere." He laughs

"Yes, I have more money than it will cost. A huge tip for you."

He sits up, sound of a huge tips makes him interested.

"Let's me just calculate," he messes around with his computer. He curses several times.

"Look I will give you five hundred and lunch at a service station."

"Deal get in." He says after a while thinking it over.

I climb in the back and put my bag next to me. We pass Southport before I realize that my ripped and bloody clothes are on the bathroom floor.

Oh well if someone finds it then clearly, I was set up as it was meant to be my ticket to freedom. He drives in silence with the radio on.

He lowers the radio down.

"So, what's a good-looking girl like yourself running away from?"

"Just taking a vacation." None of his business anyway.

"If so bad timing, the snow is meant to be coming in the next week."

"Then why are you still working?" He goes quiet that shut him up nobody knows if the snow will bring the country to a standstill.

I wake as the car comes to a stop at a service station my belly growls a little from being hungry.

I open the door and take in the fresh air. The scenery is greener and less grey from the dull city buildings.

"Come on." I say to him and he follows behind.

We end up in subway I buy him and myself a full meal.

"We going to eat in silence?" He asks I shrug and take a bite.

"Actually, can you take me to Keswick further in the lake district?"

He shrugs.

"I will give you another two hundred." I add.

"Sure, what's it like there?"

"Haven't you ever been there?"

"No," He looks over my shoulder. "I have a family, money isn't easy, so I am in my taxy all week, we don't have the luxury of holidays."

Is he trying to make me feel sorry for him as he knows I have money or is he even being honest.

"Do you have a picture of your family?" I ask him putting down my sandwich.

He takes out his wallet, opens it and slides it across to me.

"My son Charlie, my daughter Elizabeth and my wife Beth, actually do you mind me taking a call need to tell my wife I will be late home."

"No of course go ahead." Now I feel bad that I thought he was trying to get more money from me.

He stands and leaves dialling as he goes.

I finish my food and stare out the window watching the cars go by, finally he comes back.

"Sorry about that," he says. "My daughter is sick."

"Then you should go home I can make my way there." Now I feel really bad.

"No, she has been to the doctors she has one of them twenty-four-hour bugs."

"If you are sure then finish eating."

He finished eating and takes his drink with him, he climbs into the car and puts his cup in the drink holder.

He types Keswick on his navigation system and sets off.

The hills and trees pass us by its so beautiful in the countryside I prefer it here it's nice and peaceful.

We get there faster than I thought I see the sign and begin to look at how much money I have on me.

I take five thousand out for him.

"We are here." He pulls into a car park and opens the door for me.

"Thanks, here." I hand him the stack of money.

"No, I can't take that much."

"I won't take no for an answer now take it."

"How do you know I am not trying to take it, I could be trying to rob you."

I unzip my jacket I feel and hope I can trust him he seems honest, so I flash my gun.

"Trust me you couldn't take it, buy something nice or go on a holiday." I take his hand and put the cash in his palm.

Walking away he stops me.

"Hey you left this."

It's my sweatshirt must of fell out when I was searching for money I put it unfolded back in my bag and thank him.

The snow is thicker here and it's colder it takes me a while to walk to the main high Street where the shops are.

When I was here as a teen I remember it busy of course that was the summer and now it's freezing shops seem to still be open though.

I head to the church which is in the centre, it's an information desk. The bell dings as I open the door.

"Hello," A man behind the desk says. "First person in here today."

"Hi, I was wondering do you know of any places to stay?"

"All the hotels are closed because of the weather but I know a farmhouse they have a caravan I can ring them for you?"

"If it's no trouble."

"Oh no trouble at all," he picks up the phone and dials. "Hello this is Fred, how is the family?" He waits. "Good, good, well I have a young woman here who needs a place to stay but all the hotels are closed." He pauses. "Yes, I will ask her." He puts the phone to his chest. "They say you are welcome to stay there if you are willing to walk a while the roads all snowed up, so they can't pick you up?"

"Yes, I don't mind the walk."

"Okay then I will let her know," he puts the phone down. "The key is in the caravan door as they won't be in the farmhouse as they have to go get the animals in."

"Do you have a map to show me where I am going?"

He takes a map out and show me the way.

"Can I take the map?"

"Yes of course I have many of them, take care."

Now I have a long walk up a narrow road that cars can't pass on. But I suppose it could be worse I could have nowhere to stay.

The views are stunning I think I am in a valley as there's a mountain to the left and right.

The road winds and eventually I can't see anything I just follow the road blindly. I didn't pack a torch and I forgotten my tent grr.

I bump into a few hedges and fences along the way I have to pull my foot up out the snow and bring it back down to move forward it's slow going but I reach a farmhouse. It has a single bulb shining on it.

I get my phone out and use the light, cattle grid no way around, so I step carefully over it making sure my foot doesn't fall through.

I end up in a small car park another light is above the house door. I look around and find the caravan.

The snow now getting heavier I quickly head for the caravan, I reach the door and find the key in the lock. Turning it, I get pushed in as the snow tumbles inside.

The door won't close because the snow is inside. I drop my bag on the floor and go to find something. I find a brush that will have to do, I hold the snow with the brush and quickly slam the door.

It holds, and I lock it. I find light switches the caravan is spacious, I am in the kitchen, down the corridor is a spacious seating area with a TV and a small dining table.

Behind me is a bedroom with two single beds and a master bedroom, a toilet in between the two rooms with a squashed shower in a corner.

I go straight to the fire in the TV room, it's gas, so I try it three times and it finally ignites. It's still cold and feels like it's getting colder.

I take my boots off and get to work I am having a good night's sleep, so I drag the master mattress to the fire and bring the covers.

I wrap myself up on the bed and let the warmth take me, but I doze in and out of sleep as it's still cold, but it gets warmer. Like a never-ending fight between the cold and warmth.

I take a shower in the morning it's squashed, but I am glad it still works as the hot water is comforting. There's a knock on the door I change and look in the mirror straightening my sweat shirt.

I open the door to have the snow gush in I grab a women's arm as she gets pulled in with the snow.

"Hello, I am Violet I own the farmhouse glad you made it here we got worried if you got caught in the snow."

"I am Helena nice to meet you." I walk over to my bag and go to give her the money.

"Oh no, we won't be staying here," she sees the confusion on my face I thought I could stay here for a week. "Oh, sorry you don't know come."

9 WINDERMERE

She waits for me to get my boots on and takes my hand and leads me to her house.

"Helena this is my husband Ted." He looks up and nods. "Higher the volume up."

I notice then that he is listening to a radio the volume gets gradually louder.

"News alert. Anyone in the lake district area get out head south as the snow will continue. News just in Scotland is now cut off helicopters no longer able to evacuate."

"We tried getting money out the bank last night but looks like all bank accounts have been frozen until further notice." She says to me.

"Then you must take at least half of this." I grab her hand and put the money in it, so she can't refuse.

"Okay but you are coming with us we will drop you off in Windermere there's meant to be military evacuation there."

"When do we leave?"

"Get your things and meet back here in an hour we need to sort the animals out, set them free really."

It takes me longer than it should to get back to the caravan due to the thick snow, I don't know how they plan to drive through this, but I guess we are in the same boat, so I might as well stick with them until Windermere.

I gather my things clean up a little and wait. An hour passes, and I head out locking the door behind me.

"Get in." She says to me from the car window.

The car has chains on its wheels and a shovel like a plough machine to push the snow out of the way.

He starts the engine, the engine screams as he pushes it to its limits just to get the snow pushed out the way. Once we set off it's a little easier the snow gets pushed aside easily.

We head further into the mountains which I think isn't a good idea especially when looking out the window there is a huge drop to certain death.

But they both insist it's a short cut and no one knows when the snow fall will get heavier and they don't want to be stuck in Keswick if it does.

Buttermere, they tell me as I see for a brief second a small cluster of houses and two lakes either side. The road is steep and Ted curses.

"Brace yourselves." He says, and I can see his jaw clench.

We seem to pick up speed quickly and eventually we crash into a wall of snow, I am wearing my seat belt, so I only bash the back of my head on the back of the seat and the seat belt pushes into my stomach.

"We all okay?" Ted asks looking around and can see we are all okay.

His eyes fix on my chest he looks shocked, then I look down and realize my gun wasn't in the holster properly. I quickly zip up my jacket.

"Stay here I am going to check the damage." He doesn't say anything about the gun, but I knew he saw it.

He comes back several minutes later.

"The tires flat and I used the spare last week we're going have to go into the village." I climb out and my boots sink into snow.

Ugh this snow is starting to really annoy me already. But they might need help, so I follow them into the village. The scenery is beautiful even covered in snow, I can imagine the different shades of green.

We head to what looks like a barn we find no one there. Then we head to a shop I notice smoke and so do they.

Once inside we find a person hurrying with a bag.

"Clearly I am not open for business." The person behind the counter says and carries on stashing money from the cash register.

"We are looking for a spare tire, know of anywhere?" Ted asks.

"Nope I am probably the only one left in the village. Go have a look around no point staying here anyway I just burnt the last log for the fire."

We head back out.

"Go take a walk meet back here in a few hours I have to go get a few things out of the car." Ted says, and Violet follows.

It's snowing but I am not completely freezing so I take a walk to the lake, Buttermere lake I find a tunnel that's used as a path and take shelter.

I venture out and put my hand through the snow bringing out a hand full of stones. Some thin enough to skim across the lakes surface.

I watch the stones skim, hopping on the lakes surface then sink.

But I quickly go back into the tunnel as it starts to get cold and putting my hand in the snow wasn't a good Idea.

An hour passes as I just watch the snow I head through the dark tunnel and head to the meet up point.

"Catch." Ted says while throwing a bag at me and then throws two more.

One is my bag from his car the others looks like a sleeping bag and a tent that says one person.

"We have to sleep here today," Violet explains. "Takes a while to find a suitable tire and then get it up the hill to the car, so I will show you where to put the tent and then I will be back tomorrow."

She leads the way but stops at the edge of a white snow field I go to go forward, but her arm stops me.

She picks up a stick off the ground and plunges it into the snow which gives way to ditch and a stream inside it.

Violet does this several times before a thud can be heard and she starts to clear the snow either side of the bridge.

I walk carefully across as it's still a little slippery. She doesn't join me as I think by the looks of the walls I am now in the field it's all white, so I can't be certain.

I head to a tree near a wall it towers above me and hopefully should give me a little bit of shelter. I erect the tent it's quite low to the ground and it obviously is right only one person can fit in this.

The sleeping bag I quickly take out and unravel it then get it inside. It looks warm inside, but I clear a space on the ground outside and try for several minutes to light a fire.

The morning more snow has fell overnight. I see Violet in the distance coming my way.

"Morning." She says. "May I sit?"

"Sure." She sits in the tiny bit of an entrance to the tent, she hands me a cereal bar and then looks to the scenery.

"Looks beautiful doesn't it?"

"Yes," I speak in between bites. "It's very peaceful."

"Once you have ate I will help you pack up, we got the tire on last night."

We sit for a few minutes looking at the surrounding mountains majority all white. Then we re-pack the tent.

The cars parked up over the small bridge where a car park is.

I get in and throw all my bags next to me. We head up windy roads I look out the window and feel instantly sick with the massive drops and how close we are to the edge.

As we head to Windermere the snow seems to be less thick on the ground the car has less trouble moving it aside.

I noticed when I woke I slept with my guns and my ribs are in a little pain from sleeping awkwardly on the guns.

There's a checkpoint up ahead I quickly make sure I zip up my jacket this time, so no one can notice.

We get nearer, and the soldiers raise their weapons.

"Stop!" A soldier shouts but clearly, he is stating the obvious you would have to have a death wish to try and drive through a military checkpoint.

He comes to the window and shines a light in my face even though it's bright, so he could see me anyway.

"You will have to get out and walk only military vehicles allowed in the village." The soldier says.

"Can we turn around and go around the village?" Ted asks.

"Yes, you can, but we advise you to head south."

"I will get out here then." I say to them.

"Okay." Violet says to me. "Take the tent and sleeping bag and when it's all over you know where we live you should come visit."

"Thanks, and I will do."

I throw the bags around my shoulders and wave to them as they drive off. The soldier waves to his colleague down the road to let him know I'm coming.

"The soldier down their will show you the way."

Luckily the soldier doesn't pat me down probably would of if I was a guy.

The soldiers seem on alert manning machine guns on trucks, but the metal bodies of the guns are lowered like sleeping penguins. There's quite a lot of people here.

Everyone is wearing their thickest warmest winter wear. Big backpacks stood with their families or alone. Waiting for the soldiers, most soldiers walk around trying to look for trouble their guns lowered.

"In a line people." A voice booms into the silence.

I head to where some sort of line has formed.

"We are heading for Yorkshire," he pauses because of the chatter from the people. He pulls his sidearm and shoots into the air to get silence. "We are getting more evacuees and then heading to Wales. Any one that doesn't like that they can go any time."

No one argued so he spoke to a soldier telling them to get them on the back of the trucks.

I am helped onto the flatbed truck by a soldier I take my seat nearest the front just behind where the driver is.

There's three trucks that are carrying civilians and a truck at the front and back with a mounted machine gun.

The sleeping machine guns are fully alert when we set off scanning the surrounding buildings and once we leave them behind the surrounding countryside.

Snow gets sprayed to the sides as the trucks make easy work of creating a path. The snow starts to fall heavy as we leave like we got out in time.

Yorkshire here we come, but where exactly are we going I don't know. Do I care not right now I don't even know if I am safe or if they are still coming after the Orban line.

I have my pistols still in the holsters under my arms so if I must fight I will I just hope I don't get searched.

We are meant to be picking up more people I don't know where they will put them the trucks are quite full it's just enough space for our feet.

My bags are between my legs like everyone else's. No one speaks on the journey just the odd cough rings out into the silence.

There's a car abandoned in the road I can see it, the front truck speeds up and so do we. The truck slams into it forcing it to move aside.

I put my hood up as the snows starting to melt in my hair it's rather annoying. It's a cold and wet journey but the scenery isn't too bad well when you get to see it in between the snow showers.

Why is the convoy armed I think as I start to get bored? Maybe they think people will try to steal the trucks for themselves to get through the snow.

Or maybe something more serious maybe somewhere in the country one convoy has been attacked or just maybe because they just need them to pull the trucks out of thick snow if they get stuck.

10 SKIPTON

We arrive at a town called Skipton a few hours later, I think it was a few hours I didn't check my watch just in case I flashed my bracelet.

"Everybody stretch your legs. Meet back here in thirty minutes."

Oh, great what am I meant to do for half an hour on my own in a town I've never been to. Well is it a town it could be classed as a village anyway there seems to be not a lot to do here.

I hear talk of a castle and follow a group keeping my distance, so they don't try and strike a conversation with me.

We turn a corner and can see the castle instantly it looks impressive the snow hasn't hit that much here only a little bit.

We head through an entrance and pass a ticket booth. Luckily the gates aren't locked.

We head straight for the ramp that leads into the castle. Most drop their bags in the courtyard, but I look around.

There's a certain smell in here I would say like a smell of some wood preserver trying to keep the place from rotting.

I enter a bedroom decorated with all the old paintings on the wall and a four-poster bed with curtains. The wood floor creaks underneath me.

I enter another room and it's freezing but it's not different from the other rooms only there is what looks like a toilet. Well a piece of wood with a hole cut in.

No, it can't be is the cold coming from the toilet. I have to look, yep there is a hole and that goes straight into the moat that surrounds the castle.

Remind me never to live in a castle. But I have to admit the place looks very, very impressive.

There's other rooms which I quickly go around. A large Hall with a large fire place most rooms have a fire place.

Most of the rooms lead back into the courtyard where everyone is sitting around a tree in the centre.

I take a seat on some steps and finally get my bags off my shoulder. Yes, I sat in snow, but I would rather be out here sitting in the snow than inside then forget the time and be left behind.

A few soldiers enter the courtyard and take a seat. They begin checking their weapons. My weapons look brand new, so I am relying on them to work if and only if I really need to use them.

I drink some water and eat a chocolate bar from my bag.

"You there." Someone says I look around hoping it wasn't aimed at me.

Yep it was aimed at me.

"Yes?" I say covering my mouth and finishing what I ate.

"Nothing I was just wanting to hear your voice, all the rest are from here, but you have an accent."

"Oh," damn it he knows I am not from here. "Yes, I was on vacation bad timing." I force a laugh.

"Very bad timing," he says and stands up. "Time to go."

He leads the way, I follow behind it's like a duck and its babies following.

There's a few extra people on the backs of the trucks that must have arrived.

We climb onto the trucks and head off again. Again, the snow begins heavy it's almost like it's following us letting us know if we get left behind we will be covered in snow.

I already am covered in snow my pants are wet from sitting in it and so is my hair. I look strange, but I tuck my long hair into the back of my jacket so only the sides and top are exposed.

"Why can't we have a gun?" A guy asks one of the soldiers that's on the truck with us.

"Because civilians aren't allowed guns."

"But why?"

"Because it's illegal."

"But why?"

"Listen," the soldier turns to face him. "I do what I am told I don't know why that's just the law."

The person seems to understand that and goes back to looking at the white scenery like the rest of us.

It's cold but the shivering has created warmth inside my jacket which I am glad to have.

We continue driving for a long while I keep an eye on road signs if they aren't covered in snow. We pass a sign that has left turn for Liverpool. I won't be back there for a while I guess.

We head south and turn off just passed Chester. I don't know where I am, but I notice a hill or a mountain with what looks like ruins of maybe a fort on top.

We turn left over a bridge I can see a fast-flowing river underneath. We stop on the other side they say the same thing be back in an hour.

I walk away from the main group totally not a good idea, but I want to go check out those ruins.

I head back over the bridge and then behind these shops there is another bridge, but underneath is a canal.

I walk down a small lane with a walk sign pointing towards the hill. I go past a school and finally come to the base of the hill.

My bags get heavier as I head upwards, and the snow starts getting heavier. Stupid idea but I am curious, so I continue.

I reach the ruins atop the mountain; the views are stunning and the remains I can't tell what it used to be maybe a fort as it has good views of the surrounding area and the village below.

I sit on top of one of the walls to give myself a rest from the bags. The snow gets heavier and I can no longer see the village it's just white with snow.

Then there's an explosion I can see fire in the distance. What was that, why would there be an explosion. Was it an accident.

They're the thoughts that race through my mind at first. But I have to move I don't know anyone down there, so I decide it's best not to go and check either way it wasn't good.

If it was an accident the people would still fight for who gets to sit on the trucks and if it wasn't an accident well I don't need to explain why it would be a bad idea to go back.

I put my bags back on my shoulders and un-zip my jacket and bring out one of my guns, silencer already attached.

I head quickly back down the hill across the lane and I head East using the canal path. A twig snaps in the woods to my left I spin and hold up my gun. It's a woman she is holding a gun.

"Don't!" I say as their weapon isn't pointed at me and they definitely aren't from the army convoy.

They hesitate. But then she goes to raise the weapon. I squeeze the trigger they drop in the woods. I carry on I need to get far away from here even if I used a silencer her friends will be along shortly.

My hair clings to my forehead I have to tuck it back behind my ear several times. I have been running well if it can be classed as running as all the gear slows me down, but I know that I need them no matter how tired I am.

Sometimes there are patches of snow that slow me down even more. So annoying but I carry on I have no idea where, but I think I am heading North East as we were heading South East.

A shot rings behind me but why. I take a left off the canal path and decide to go cross country. Slower going but I think they won't follow me.

I hit the first barbed wire fence and manage to get my leg over the fence. Bad idea I hear a snag and immediately stop.

My jeans are stuck on the barbed wire near my thigh. If I turn a wrong direction it might go into my skin and that's not good the infection will probably kill me.

I slowly reach down, slowly to feel the barbed wire it's only tugging at my jeans. So, I keep hold of my jeans and pull, a small hole appeared but at least my skin is still intact.

Close call. Quickly move on. Open field but I get across quickly without trouble. To be honest I think I am safe.

I slow down I still want to put some distance between them and me and I can't be certain that I am free.

I am now drenched in sweat, and I haven't changed my clothes. The tent I put up under a tree and change. I only have like two pairs of everything so next time I will have to find a river or re-wear everything but that's the future.

Now I eat. The wind rustles the trees above me a calming sound. The ground also stirs with the wind. It's peaceful if it wasn't freezing and the circumstances where different I would happily spend more time here.

I stop eating my mouth open, is that a stream I can hear. I follow the sound down a slope. It is a stream not enough to wash clothes, but I fill my bottle and wash my face holding my hair back. More water is needed to tackle my greasy hair.

I get into my sleeping bag, brush my hair and rest my head.

I don't sleep just the thought what happened back there. Why was it attacked and are they still following me?

I pack quickly and head off again. I find my gloves and put them on as it's starting to get cold, really cold and my fingers are useless at the moment.

I sleep when it gets dark as I can't see anything stumbling around in the dark with barbed wire fences, not such a good idea.

The sun comes up I pack and climb a fence and come across a long ditch. Nope not a ditch under the snow my foot hits tarmac I think it's tarmac. Looks like a road.

I head along the road and find a sign pole covered with snow, I wipe it away the sign reads: Moel Famau.

Looking where the sign is pointing it looks like a single lane, country road probably my better option than this open main road so I head that way.

A shot rings off in the distance hopefully a farmer.

The road gets steeper and hills rise to my left and right. I pass a car park I can see this sign it's a toilet block I head there to get out of the snow that's now swirling all around me.

They said the snow was going to be bad but not this bad where I am now forced to hide inside a toilet block.

Once the snow stops a little I keep straight on the road. There's two car parks now one on my left and one on the right.

The road leads down to a valley I think it's a valley as there is mountains again all on the other side.

I walk down the steep road slowly, so I don't trip and tumble all the way down.

It's warmer down here I say warmer but really, it's just less cold. Yes, less cold and less windy, my hair doesn't try to whip me in the face.

I need to find somewhere to rest trekking through this snow is burning my thighs and taking the majority of my energy.

It's quite odd the silence now like I know it's countryside just crazy compared to the city don't get me wrong I prefer the quiet still air. Still air well it is being pushed around by the strong winds.

11 GIRL

There's a barn. I am excited to see it. But is it empty.

I head towards the barn, over a field. My boot gets stuck and I go face first into the snow my arms don't stop me as they just sink into the snow and eventually I feel the dirt.

I jump back onto my feet and brush the snow off my face.

I head for a bush overlooking the barn. There is no farm house which is a bonus if I don't see anyone then they would have to come by car if they wanted to check up on their barn.

I wait in the bush for an hour maybe two no movement and I can't feel my noes, so I head in. There's a lock on the door, I fumble for my gun and shoot the lock.

I take out both guns and head on in, I don't know what's inside. It smells like hay a little bit of stale air, but I check everywhere even up the ladders, no one is here.

I put my tent on a small platform only accessible by the ladders. Inside a barn, inside a tent should keep me warm as it's still cold in here.

Only problem I have with my clothing is when I open my jacket you probably can see my pink sweatshirt amongst all the white snow. But hey I like the colour the other is beige, but I have worn that already. I should have packed more.

I should have packed a lot more things but again I can't sit here thinking of what I should have done. Just have to move forward.

It's getting colder and my teeth begin to chatter I can't light a fire up here amongst the hay, so I head down the ladders and clear a space on the floor. I gather hay and light it.

The warm is like a welcome hello it touches my skin and eventually my teeth stop chattering.

I can't leave it un-attended so I put it out once I am warm and quickly scramble up the ladder into my sleeping bag, it's also warm in here but I am not taking any clothing off tonight I will just sleep in it.

I wake, and I can start to smell my clothing smells damp from sweat. How was I sweating during the night when it's freezing I may never know the answer, although sleeping with clothing on probably wasn't the best choice.

At least when I get out the snows stopped, and the sky is clear. I can now see further ahead, the mountains around me it's really beautiful but the snows still there on the ground reminding me it will be back.

It gets to lunch time before the clouds roll in and I am walking blind in a whiteout. I can't stop to eat what little I have as I can't see my hand in front of my face. I don't want to risk things falling out of my bag or leaving my tent behind.

I slip and trip. One hand grabs my bag the other tries to stop myself from falling.

My hand touches something that makes me stop. Is that. My hand investigates yes it feels like a body.

I can feel their chest, but my hand goes higher up trying to make sure it is a human and then my hand touches their chin.

I retract my hand quickly sickened I didn't think it was possible I am in the middle of nowhere.

I don't know if there are any more bodies, I don't want to trip and fall onto one, so I stay put. Yes, it is a stupid idea as I am in a whiteout and I am now slowly starting to freeze to death.

I use my feet to scan around me to see if anything is close. Nothing there so I sit. At first the snow melts and I can feel the cold coming through my multiple layers.

I curl up into a ball and rest my head on my bag. I thought I would only wait here a few more minutes but the whiteout had taken more energy from me, so when I woke I find a thin layer of snow on top of me. Luckily, I'm alive but I'm cold to the bone.

My hands find the ground and I push to get onto my feet, most of the snow falls off as I stand I brush the remainder off.

I turn around the whiteout has gone now, and I can see the bodies two of them a man and women. By their proximity to each other they died together caught in the cold.

I head on down the path. Further down I stop and sit on a log, it's not as cold now and it's stopped snowing, so I take off my gloves and lower my hood and take out my brush.

My hair needs to be brushed trust me I am stressed right now, and it calms me. I brush out the knots and put my gloves back on.

I carry on down the path, the path fades and turns into a wooded area, ugh then snow begins again.

The snow is not as bad as I thought the trees keep most of it at bay but in the shade, it's even colder.

I freeze like a deer. There's a person up ahead a teenager maybe I don't know. They haven't spotted me, so I dive left behind a tree.

I can see them better here, a girl maybe. She looks five feet in height a little bit smaller than me, her blonde hair is what caught my eye. She is shivering uncontrollably, and her hands look frozen in place.

What do I do? Do I intervene, or does she have family nearby that have gone to gather fire wood?

I watch her for a while making sure it's not too long before even I couldn't help her. I decide to help her.

I walk slowly out of the tree line showing I am unarmed, I am unarmed but I have my weapons in the holsters in case it's a trap.

She doesn't even react her eyes move to look at me, but her neck doesn't follow.

She's just perched on a log unable to move. I won't be able to find dry firewood to create a fire for her.

I noticed her hands are exposed to the cold, she must not have gloves, so I take mine off and put them carefully on her hands.

I notice she's just wearing a top and a jacket no sweat shirt she will freeze to death in her current state.

"We are going to hug," I say. "Move your eyes up and down if you understand." Her eyes move.

"Ok I am going to unzip your jacket and put my arms around you and hug, I want you to try do the same." Her eyes move up and down.

Her hands move around my stomach clumsily as they are still clearly frozen. Her hands miss the holsters luckily as I don't want her to panic right now.

"This is the most awkward position I have been in." I say after hugging her for a while. I read somewhere warming the chest warms the rest, don't know if it's true but I must try warm her up.

One corner of her mouth lifts to smile but it drops as her face still looks a little frozen.

My head is getting colder, I need to take more drastic action. I get my spare sweatshirt.

"We need to put our heads together." She quickly does it, I nearly get brain freeze off how cold she is.

I wrap the spare sweatshirt around both our heads, really, I don't know if it will work I just hope my remaining warmth and the sweatshirt will work together to get her warm.

After a while I feel her fingers cling more tightly around me.

"My name's Grace by the way," she says eventually.

"Nice to meet you. I am Helena." I say

She seems warm enough after a little while, so that we can stop awkwardly hugging.

"Where do you sleep?" I ask looking around finding nothing.

"We don't. We kept travelling trying to find the next village we aren't prepared."

"Where's your parents?"

"They should have been back by now." Distress in her voice.

"Which way did they go?" I ask ready to go find them for her.

"That way." She says pointing.

I go to take a step but realize that's the way I came from, where the two bodies lie in the cold.

"What did they look like?" I ask hoping they didn't look like them two.

She describes them perfectly not faltering, not missing a detail, happy as she remembers them and then asks, "Why?"

Do I lie to her and save her the pain or tell her the truth, I haven't been in a situation where I care a lot about someone's feelings.

I decide the truth, so I sit down next to her and explain. She starts crying, she stands up, but I can't have her wandering off to look for them she would freeze to death, so I wrap my arms around her.

She hits me at first but eventually gives up and cries into my jacket.

We stand there for a while until she can't cry anymore, and all her tears are gone.

"I have to get the tent out, you can help me put it up." She doesn't say anything.

We get the tent up quickly before darkness hits there isn't any time to hunt for any firewood.

"Here it's my pink sweatshirt." I remembered before she was only wearing a t-shirt she needs an extra layer even if her jacket looks thick. "I have worn it, so sorry if it smells, it might be a little big."

She quickly takes off her jacket and hands it to me and slips the sweatshirt over her head and pulls out her pony tail.

I pull out my sleeping bag and realize I only have one, I look at Grace and hand it to her.

She takes off her boots and climbs into the tent it's going to be cramped as it's only for one person.

I take one last look at the surrounding woods and join her, I accidently land on her foot I say sorry then quickly move over.

My face is squashed onto the tents side, I can feel her breath on my neck and sleeping on the floor isn't comfortable.

I don't sleep all night as Grace tosses and turns putting her arms on my face or an elbow in my ribs.

I end up with an arm and somehow a leg flung over me the sleeping bag zip must have failed. She wakes up but is still silent.

We walk for a few days even in another whiteout and she still doesn't speak.

It's must be the seventh day that she speaks to me.

"Can I borrow your hair brush?" She asks me quietly as she can see me brushing my hair.

"Sure," I say and hand it over. "So, you plan to stick with me?" I ask and bite my tongue as I don't know if it's too soon, stupid, or both.

She stops brushing her hair and looks at me like I am stupid. "I am twelve years old, I am not stupid I need an adult."

"You seem quite older, like in the head I mean."

She carries on brushing her hair. "I know everyone always says it to me."

"Well anyway I will look after you, you can stick with me."

"How do I know you won't just leave me in the woods?"

Good point I am a total stranger to her, I think to myself.

"Well I haven't for several days. What if I give you something of mine?" She puts down the brush and looks at me, so I carry on, "This bracelet it's expensive, I bought it this year, but it still means a lot to me." I slip it off and hand it to her.

"So, you mean if I wear it you will always be near me?"

"Yep and if you ever got lost I will always come looking for you."

She slips it onto her wrist it suits her.

12 CONWY

As we walk we take turns wearing my gloves, so her hands don't freeze. We reach a stream; the water looks clean and fresh, so I go to one knee and reach into the water with my bottle.

My fingers just about touch the water's surface and it's even colder than the cold trying to freeze me to death. I take a sip and hand it to Grace.

"So, where's all your gear?"

"We were on holiday, we went for a day out and got lost in a forest."

"Get down." I quickly pull her down with me, I can hear people talking on the road above us. One steps on the roads edge, it flakes off covering us in dust and snow.

"The stream is just down there; can't we take a rest?"

I pull out my gun I can feel Graces eyes on me.

"No, we aren't stopping." They walk off I give a sigh of relief and holster my gun.

"Let's move on." I say to her.

"Aren't you going to explain?" She asks as she follows.

"What's there to say I have guns two of them."

"They are the most illegal thing in the country."

"Actually-" She interrupts me.

"Just tell me or I am not going anywhere with you." She says and folds her arms.

"Okay." I tell her everything that has happened the words just seep out of me. When I finish she hugs me, I am totally confused I don't know why she is hugging me.

I hug her back it makes me feel, well it makes me feel warm inside like all the coldness around us is gone.

After hugging for several long minutes, we carry on. Even though she takes big gulps of my water and takes my comfy sleeping bag and borrows my hair brush for long amounts of time she is growing on me, I am glad I met her, of course I am sad of the circumstances we met.

"We need to find you some gear." I say as we pull ourselves through the thick snow.

"Where from? There's nothing around."

"I know." I admit I haven't seen any proper groups of buildings in a while.

We walk for what must be a week, we walk mainly on single country lanes. We see no signs of life just a lot of snow.

Still no shops just farm houses but no point going near them, most have a single candle light visible. The occupants probably waiting it out on alert for looters.

I hold her hand when the whiteout hit she doesn't object as we don't want to lose each other.

We must have wandered off onto a field as the ground underneath the snow feels different and there aren't walls either side.

I find a sign post and wipe the snow off, it reads: Conwy five miles. Not that far could be worse.

I can't judge how long it will take to walk that far as trying to walk through knee high snow isn't easy.

We may be close but there's a forest we are going to have to head through.

"Will you teach me to shoot?" Grace asks behind me.

"Never." I say quickly trying to put an end to it.

"But why?"

"Like you said they are illegal," she doesn't object. "Stay right behind me and keep your ears open."

"Well I can't close my ears." She says quietly which makes me smile.

A quiet shout escapes her as I suddenly stop causing her to walk into me.

"Keep even closer." I whisper.

We go behind a tree and crouch, the snows stopped so I can now see more clearly.

There's two military vehicles with a line of soldiers, I hear a loud shout saying "Halt," but the rest I can't hear.

They are shouting to a small group of people at one end of the bridge, the small group seem to possess weapons behind their backs.

A twig snaps behind us I pull out one gun.

"Grace it's important you listen." I put the gun in her hand and wrap her other hand around it. "Point and shoot."

"But…" She looks at me, she looks scared.

"It'll be okay." I say and give her arm a reassuring squeeze.

I take out the second gun, if the military starts firing the group might run this direction and I am not taking chances.

The guns go off I can see the flashing as the triggers are squeezed. Grace goes to look but I make sure she's looking behind.

Something happens behind me, before I can turn Grace squeezes the trigger. Sounds like the bullet hit a tree.

"Come here girls." A taunting voice comes from the forest.

Grace is frozen, maybe not the best choice of words. I pull the gun out of her hands and throw her almost in front of me.

"Head for the military on the bridge." I hope they don't shoot us.

I holster my weapons, so they are out of sight, Grace is slowing probably the winter gear is making her too hot or heavy.

I look over my shoulder to see a group of men chasing us.

"Run." A soldier in front shouts.

State the obvious.

Grace reaches the line of soldiers. I turn now I know she is safe, I take out my weapons and drop to one knee.

I take out as many as I can before the soldiers join in just as the group return fire.

"Hold your fire." Their commander shouts as the last one drops.

I run to find Grace, but I am stopped by a soldier.

"Let her through."

Grace runs to me and gives me a tight hug, I stroke her head for comfort, I guess I am new to this I never thought I would have to look after someone else.

"Follow me." Their commander says.

We walk down a single track that's been cleared probably by the military vehicles.

We walk the length of the bridge; the castle is the first thing my eyes gaze upon getting bigger and bigger. Grace doesn't turn her head when we come to a stop.

"So," the man says. "How do you two know each other?"

"Sisters," I say. "Can't you tell?"

He looks at us both, scratches his beard. "Actually, I can now, you both have similar stunning looks in a non-creepy way of course."

"Thanks." I guess.

"I would normally take your weapons off you and lock you up, but we could do with a skilled shooter like yourself."

"I'll be happy to help."

He walks us to a house that is opposite the castle, he takes off his coat and puts more logs on the fire and pokes it with a stick, the fire comes back to life.

Grace went straight to it and began warming her hands.

"I'll find you a house, but we are only staying here for a month before the worst of the snow hits, we will be heading to Cornwall," he picked up his coat again. "I'll be back in an hour."

I ask Grace to move over and sit next to her on the floor. The warmth touches my skin it feels good to be truly warm again.

The commander knocks before entering his own home.

"Catch." I catch, they are keys. "Your new house, follow me."

As we walk he tells me what's what, the castle and the walls that surround the village are off limits to civilians but as I will help defend I am allowed.

"My men will be given your description just say Sergeant Crater has authorized it."

He took us through a high street which was just one Street, where he said most of shops where located, some open, most closed.

We enter the main residential area where he leads us to a cottage on the corner.

"It is or was a holiday cottage no one was staying in it so it's all yours. Come find me in the castle tomorrow."

I hand the keys to Grace, so she has the honours, instinct tells her to reach for the light switch. It works the light turns on, I'm surprised.

I turn to ask the sergeant, but it seemed like he had disappeared into the fresh snow storm.

I'll ask him tomorrow, I close the door and leave the cold outside as the fire has already been lit and there's logs ready to be put onto it.

I head upstairs to check the bedroom situation fresh bedding by the looks of it, I head to the master bedroom where there's a blanket I take it with me downstairs.

I take off my jacket and boots and sit next to Grace as soon as I get comfy Grace places her head on my lap.

I put the blanket over the both of us trying not to disturb her.

Sleep doesn't take me I keep thinking was it irresponsible of me to give a twelve-year-old a gun, even if she does act much older.

Sleep must take me eventually as when I wake I find Grace gone and the contents of my bag sprawled out on the floor.

I head upstairs trying to find her and only find her clothes at the top and pick them up, but I hear her shout from downstairs.

"I am down here." She shouts.

She's sitting on a chair with a tiny mirror trying to fix her hair.

"Where did you get the bath robe from?" I ask and realize I am holding a wet towel that was amongst her clothes. "And does the shower work?"

"The robes are in the cupboard under the sink and yes it does but please help me first." She says holding the brush out to me.

I sort her hair out and tie it up in a ponytail, once done she takes her clothes back.

"There isn't a washing machine." She says and heads upstairs she comes back down wearing the same clothes the top she is wearing is starting to smell but it's hard to wash anything.

I head to the shower. I turn it on and leave my hand under the warm running water for several minutes, the water is feels good. I climb in the shower, I could stay here all day, but the sergeant told me to meet him.

"Sit." Grace says when I come down the stairs brush in hand.

"So, are you coming to meet the sergeant with me?"

"Yes, if you dint mind he thinks we are sisters, so he won't mind, will he?"

"He shouldn't do."

There is a knock on the door Grace goes to see who it is.

"It's the sergeant."

I run up the stairs to get dressed. He knocks several times so Grace lets him in. I hear Grace tell him I will be down soon.

I put on my dirty clothes and make sure my guns are fully loaded and head downstairs.

"Ah, there you are, I was in this section thought we might as well walk to the castle."

"Lead the way." I put on my jacket just as the cold hits when the doors opened a reminder of the situation.

"Wait." Grace says and steps behind me, she gathers my hair and ties it up with a hair band from around her wrist.

"Thanks." I say and kiss her on the cheek. "Let's go." We get outside and the damn sergeant disappeared into the snow again. "Sergeant Crater." I shout.

He appears the way I thought he went.

"What is it?"

"Let us catch up to you." I can't remember which way it is to the castle and I can't even see that far ahead as the snow won't stop."

He takes us through a shop which leads to a bridge and then into a winding slope that goes upwards.

The castle wall looms over us. Grace falls a little behind still staring at the castle with fascination.

The sergeant disappears but this time I know he is just in front somewhere in the castle. I pass a soldier as I pass through the entrance.

"Stop." I hear behind me and find Grace being stopped by a soldier. "Crater why's this girl here?"

The sergeant looks at me. "She's with me." I say quickly.

"Let her through then," he picks up a clipboard and starts walking." So, as you can start to hear we have generators hooked up to the village It's why we have lights."

"But why do you need me?" I ask as I am very curious.

"I am happy to look past the fact that you are a trained killer only because I lost a few men kidnapped or maybe just wandered off to far and got lost."

"Aren't you a trained killer?"

He stops and looks at me. "Okay you are a professional killer anyone can see that by your custom weapons with suppressors, but you look like the classy type only kill for good money not like the kids wanting to be in gangs. So, I know we are all safe especially as you have your sister with you."

"What do you want of me?"

"I'm going to a campsite up the hill to see if any civilians are up there. I don't want to risk losing the village, so it will be just me and you if you agree?"

"And my sister? She is safer with me."

"Sure."

"Then yes, I will help you, what do you want me to do today?"

"Walk the walls of the village keep an eye out if see if you can see anything from up there. Have a wander around you'll find your way."

13 CAMPSITE

We head a direction that one of the guards told us was the beginning of the walls, you'll easily find the stairs he said but nope. Maybe on a summers day.

"STOP!" I grab Grace and bring her to the ground, the snow cleared enough for me to see the edge of the harbour.

I pick up a stone and throw it into the, well where I think there's water it makes a splash.

"Thanks." She says, and we carry on aware that to our right there's almost certain death as it would be hard to warm yourself up when you're wet to the bone.

There's this small house to our left but also what looks like a medieval wall, we lose track of it as it's goes behind these small houses.

We reach one of the gatehouses, there's a guard and some fire.

"Ah, Helena went the wrong way, should have turned left up there but you can go out behind me," He points in the direction, "follow the street then there should be another gate with a guard he can tell you where to go."

"Can we get some warmth first?"

"Oh yeah sure."

We both quickly put our hands above the fire, feel the warmth on our faces. We stay there for a good few minutes before we decide we might as well carry on.

We find the guard, but the gate is left open, he said he heard us coming I doubt it.

He shows us the stairs to the wall, some small alley with the wall one side and a shop wall the other.

I grab the hand rail and hold on as the stairs are so slippery I almost fall back down at least four times before we finally reach the top. Left or right.

Grace says right so we go right visibility is basically zero, we walk through a small archway down some stairs then the ground is flat but seems to be on a hill going down.

We bump into a rail stopping us from falling off the edge and I realize that we are above where we warmed our hands, I look down and can see the red glow from the fire.

So, we head back the way we came and go left instead, holding the hand rail constantly the snow goes every so often, so we can see the left and right side of us is just ground, either death or serious injury if we fell over the sides.

I grab hold of Grace who nearly falls completely on her back she says thanks in a shaky voice.

We get to the worst part it's like walking up a high hill it gets higher and higher until we reach a tower.

"Should we go up?" Grace asks.

"No, we'll carry on." I say looking at the Tower, it's tiny winding steps that look completely iced over, I am not risking Graces life just to satisfy the sergeant, can't see anything from up here anyway the constant snow blocks the view.

We carry on left past the tower it goes downhill here but I slip on my back and quickly cling to the rail, Grace rushes as fast as she can to my side.

The winds knocked out of me and my back hurts, I get helped up by Grace who asks if I am okay.

"I am fine go ahead." I say so she doesn't worry but I need a lie down my back hurts.

I let her go ahead so if she falls I can at least try to catch her.

We get to a modern set of stairs that wind downwards this is where the wall seems to end. There's a train station next to us and a guard underneath guards another entrance.

"Is that you Helena?" A voice from the masked soldier.

"Yes, how do I get back to the village?"

"There's more wall to walk on but I've got word you can head back home. Behind you there's a path it goes between houses you'll find the way."

We head that way, but any path has been taken by the snow it just all looks the same but luckily there's a wall either side, I guess a path we find must lead out into a street, now I know where we are our house is around the corner.

We get in and immediately feed the fire to get the house warm before taking off our jackets.

I flop onto the couch and instantly regret it my back still hurts from that fall.

"Are you sure you're okay?" Grace asks seeing the pain on my face.

"I just bruised my back, I didn't want you to worry."

"Sit up." She says grabbing pillows and places them behind my back.
"Thanks." I say with a smile.

The sergeant arrives in the morning I hear his car first, my backs much better so I still want to go even though Grace keeps saying I should rest.

He's in an armoured jeep I can see it through the windows he beeps once I gather my things I think we should need in case things go wrong, a tent, spare clothes for me and Grace, two days of water for me and Grace.

"Unfortunately, I wasn't given a jeep with a machine gun on top." He says when I climb into the seat next to him.

"For the best, it would be colder in here if the roof was constantly open." Grace says from the back seat.

He puts the heater on and drives, we head out of a narrow road under a bridge and then away from the castle it feels strange now to be out of the village walls.

We head up winding roads past abandoned cars and up a steep hill. We carry on the road for a little longer before turning off it, I notice a sign, but it's covered in snow.

We reach the top where a reception is.

"Ah damn it." He says and punches the steering wheel, "The barrier is closed we'll have to walk from here."

We gather our gear and go under the metal barrier. He loads his weapon and checks the chamber. "You never know what we'll come across." He adds.

It's a camping and caravan site there's tents and caravans dotted over the fields. The tents look like odd shaped igloos with the snow on top of them.

"There's no one here." I whisper to him, why am I even whispering.

"This site is big, let's split up meet me at the bottom near a house you can't miss it," he walks into the tree line and turns his head. "Good luck."

The way he says it sends shivers down my spine or is it the cold.

We follow the road and go right to a section of the site, no one's there so we carry on the road as it slopes downwards, guess we are going the right way.

We spot a house at the bottom but to the right there's a field. I suppose we should go check it out.

This field seems to be filled with tents, there's a few cars but the rest must have used them to try to quickly get away. But why leave their tent.

"Grace, you first." I say jokingly as we reach the first tent.

"I don't think so." She says and opens my bag and hands me my torch. "You're meant to be looking after me, remember."

I brush the snow off the tent and unzip it, I'm surprised the snow hasn't made it cave in. It's pitch black, I flick the switch on the torch covering the tent in light. No one inside only unzipped, abandoned sleeping bags.

"There must be thirty tents, I'm not checking them all." I say to Grace and start shouting. "Anyone here?"

"Is that wise?" Grace asks.

She's right I take out my gun and continue. "Hello, hello." No one here at all. We continue and stop outside a shower block where we hear rustling coming from inside. "Stay here."

"I'm safer with you." Grace quickly replies and reaches for my hand, so I take her hand and keep her behind me. She takes over the torch and shines it in front of me.

The rustling stops as our boots crunch the snow.

I hear claws, but my mind doesn't register it and an animal shoots past us causing us both to jump in fright.

We turn to head out but the snow storms back and now we can't even see where we came from.

"We'll make a fire in here and go and find the sergeant when the snow stops."

Grace takes a nap while we wait, she rests her head on my lap.

I keep the fire under control, so the smoke doesn't kill us, or the flames don't burn the place down.

The door was left open. Bad idea it just makes it colder and the snows blowing in.

The snow eventually stops coming in. Hopefully that means the storms stopped.

"Grace wake up." I say shaking her gently, she sits up, so I can stand. Yep the snow storms stopped although the snow hasn't stopped completely.

We make our way slowly through the fresh snow to the road and head further down to the house where I hope the sergeant is.

I don't see him anywhere.

"Hey you two." A voice behind us. The Sergeant who seems to be in a pub. "Come in."

We head in. He's got a fire going and he has clearly been drinking.

"Want some?" He asks holding out a rum bottle.

"No thanks, I got to take care of this one." I say and nudge Grace who smiles back. "Can we get out of here before another snow storm hits?"

"Well I'm a bit tipsy, I don't want to crash."

"Give me the keys. I'm sure you can give me a crash course, I took a few lessons and I'm a quick learner."

"Hmm," he sips his rum. "If there's an empty field then sure. Put the fire out and let's go."

I poke the fire until it's fully extinguished. We get outside where the Sergeant throws an empty bottle against the wall.

"No." I say to him and take the full bottle off him that's he's just took out of his pocket. "You're not having anymore. Where's your weapon?"

"Ah." He says and runs back into the bar and comes out with his weapon.

I take that off him as well. "I'll give you it back when you've sobered up a little. I don't want you accidently shooting Grace or me."

We head back up the hill to the armoured vehicle, we make our way up the winding road.

When we get there, we have to scrape the fresh snow off the vehicle and carefully roll it into a nearby field, so the sergeant can teach me.

14 PSYCHOPATH

I sit in the driving seat, hands on the steering wheel, feet on the pedals. "Now what?"

"Turn the key for a start, put it in gear." I turn the key as he pulls the hand break and we start to roll forward. "Press the break." I can't remember what pedal it is.

I panic at first and press the wrong pedal and the car jolts forward. Eventually I find the right one.

After what feels like a decade I finally get sort of used to driving and the sergeant tells me to drive onto the road and head for the castle.

The snow starts and now I've got to find the window wipers. First, I accidently turn on the headlights then find the right one.

"Do you know how to work the heater? It's freezing." Grace asks blowing warm air into her hands.

Now that, I do know how to do.

The sergeant fell asleep as soon as we got onto the road.

"Wake up, we are near the entrance. If they don't see you in the vehicle they'll think I stole it and shoot at us."

"It's bullet proof." He says more clearly.

The castle and its walls are clearly visible as we drive around the winding roads. It's hard to keep my eyes on the road.

We near the entrance where a few guards are waiting under a bridge next to the castle. They wave is through.

I drop him off at his house opposite the castle. He's drunk so I put his arm around me and take him inside.

I close the door after leaving him and realize I've got the keys to his vehicle. I'll give them to him tomorrow.

I carry Graces bag for her as she looks tired, I'm also tired, I don't even know what time it is.

We slowly make our way home. Great someone has kicked in the front door. I put mine and Graces bag on the floor and take out my gun.

"Grace wait here, shout if you need me."

The doors lock is completely broken. I go through the house, no one is here luckily. They've robbed my clothes that where on my bed. Weird.

"Did they steal anything?" Grace asks as she comes inside.

"Only my clothes. You need to go check if they stole anything of yours."

She comes back after checking. "Yes, they stole my clothes that I left here. Are you going to report it?"

"In the morning. Help me move this couch to bar the door."

The couch does a good job of keeping the door shut as it's jammed between the door and the stairs. The only downside is that I have to climb over the couch to get to the stairs.

There's banging on the door in the morning, which wakes me.

"Grace." I say gently to wake her up. "I need your help with the couch."

Still half asleep she walks the stairs and begins to push the couch as I begun to pull it.

The person knocks but this time the door flies open.

"What is it?" I ask.

"The sergeant wants you. Grab all your gear." We do and follow him. "Guess you got your clothes robbed?"

"Yes, but why?"

"Don't know. We think there's a psychopath he or she robbed everyone's clothes and burnt them at the pier. We found what was left last night."

Strange. Maybe that's how it starts, the person saying I'm here, I've been in your home and then bam people start dying.

The thought sends shivers down my spine. I just want to get out of here now.

He takes us to the castle where everyone is busy. All the soldiers have their hands full with boxes.

"Helena." The sergeant says while ticking items off a clipboard. "We are moving out a few days early, but I'm sure you are aware of the situation?"

"Yes, the clothes?"

"Yes, but not just that. A few sheep's heads were found close to the main gate. Chain of command thinks there will be deaths next they say we should move south now, not to wait for any more people."

"It sounds like there's a but?"

"But," he says. "I am not going with the main convoy. Chain of command wants me to head into colder territory to a village past Betws-y-Coed and get temperature readings. Would you come with us?"

"I don't think it would be wise. I need to keep my sister safe." I say but I can feel Grace trying to get my attention. She takes my hand and leads me out of earshot of the sergeant.

"Can we go with him please? You'll keep me safe." She senses my hesitation. "Besides, the person that done these strange things may be inside these walls and may carry on their weird ways when the convoy stops to sleep." Grace makes a good point.

"Okay, but you stay even closer to me." She nods, and we walk back to the sergeant to say yes even though I already said no. "We'll join you."

"Good. We will leave later this afternoon, once the main convoy leaves. It will be cramped as we are only allowed the one vehicle."

Well I said no then yes so, I can't really change my mind just because it's going to be a little cramped.

The sergeant gives me no orders only that he'll find us when we should leave.

Grace and I head for the harbour and sit on the floor with our legs dangling above the ocean. Probably not the best idea considering we would die if we fell in.

We sit in silence throwing stones onto the ocean's surface, in the end it turns into a game of who can get there's the furthest.

"What's your favourite colour?" I ask Grace after we both grow tired of trying to beat the other.

"Probably red or an ocean blue, but the red has to be like a dark red. How about you?"

"I like black, but I also like pinks sometimes and purples."

Before we continue there's a honk of a horn on the road behind us.

I turn my head, it's the armoured vehicle. The sergeants sat at the wheel.

"Come on let's go." He says.

At least when the back-passenger door is opened the heat from inside touches my face.

There's already two in the back which is usually meant for three and now the two of us have to climb in, so yeah it will be cramped.

I sit in the middle, so Grace can look out the window. We head out the village the same way we did when we went to that campsite.

Luckily, we head past it and carry on down the road. The snow plough on the front makes easy work of the snow on the road.

There's no one out here, well I can't see anyone, I'm sure if there is they would be hold up in a house by a fire. The thought gives me goose bumps that we may be being watched.

I wish I was hold up near a fire. Actually, no I don't, I like adventures. Yes, I know I like adventures, but I need to be careful as I'm not just looking out for myself anymore.

The sergeant announces we are at Betws-y-Coed, but the bridge is blocked with a lot of snow.

"Right everyone out, except Grace." The sergeant says. He heads to the boot and gets a bunch of spades and shovels.

We have to manually move the snow it is an inconvenience.

"Now be careful, the weight of the snow might have made the bridge unstable." He adds.

Great a bridge that might be unstable and we are standing on top of it.

We finally move all the snow and climb tiredly back into the car.

We head over the bridge and out of the village and go through a forest area where we can hear a loud rushing of a waterfall through the tiny gap in the passenger window.

The scenery is quite stunning around here, I know now why Graces head has been glued to the window the whole time.

I bet it looks even more nice around here in the summer when there's no snow, then there would be all sorts of greens.

"We're here." The sergeant announces as we enter a village, he stops the vehicle just before another bridge that's blocked by snow.

"We'll have to go on foot from here. Helena, Grace you can stay in the car we'll be gone three hours at most."

At least it's warm, but what will we do for a day in the car there's not even music on the radio.

Grace climbs into the front passenger seat as soon as they leave and begins searching in the glove compartment.

"What are you up to?" I ask and climb into the driver's seat next to her.

"Got it," she says. "They are soldiers, there must have been a pack of cards somewhere."

We play card games until it goes dark, we decide not to turn any lights on even if we are in a bullet and bomb proof vehicle.

We decide to try get some sleep when it goes completely dark. I let Grace take the back seat, so she can lie down.

15 SAVIOUR

I wake with a stiff neck and an uncomfortable back. I look at Grace and it's worth it she looks comfortable.

There's a snow storm raging outside, I'm glad we've got the cars heaters.

There's a loud smacking sound, it came from outside. It makes me jump and makes Grace wake up.

I look at where the sound came from and there's a hand print on the window.

I put on my jacket, take out my gun and reach for the door handle and push it open.

It's one of the soldiers lying in the snow. He looks dead.

I peel his mask from his mouth which is frozen in place.

Once it's removed I check for signs of life. But I don't think he's breathing, his chest doesn't rise and fall.

I check for a pulse; his skin is cold a sort of dead cold. I continue to check for a pulse but can't find one.

"Is he dead?" Grace asks from within the car.

"I think so." I reply.

"You're not sure. You need to help him if you're not sure." Grace adds.

"I mean yes, he's not breathing and he's far too cold, plus there's no signs of life." Just to make sure I try to find a heartbeat but nothing. "And I can't feel his heart beat."

I try pumping his chest but after a while I realize there's no point he's gone.

He's got no bullet holes in him, I suppose that's a good thing. Looks like exhaustion and the cold got him.

But then blood appears and turns the snow rose red, looks like he might have fell and broke his ankle and bashed his head.

There's not much I can do so I head back into the car out of the cold.

"Now what?" Grace asks. "The sergeant is still out there."

Before I can answer the sergeants, voice is on the radio.

"Helena are you there?" The radio goes silent how do I answer him? "There's a button on the receiver." He adds, his voice sounds like he is in pain.

"Hello." I say finding the button.

"Good you're there." The sergeant says giving a sigh of relief. "I'm hurt, I've broke a leg and I think one of my fingers is lost, maybe some of my toes."

"What do you want me to do?" I ask, Grace shakes her head at me. What did I do? Oh. "I mean how do I help?"

"You'll have to come get me, I'm in a cave. There's a stream to your left, you'll hear it when you get out of the vehicle if it's not frozen. Follow it keep it to your left, head over a bridge, then keep it to your right, then it should take you to the cave and you'll need some rope."

"Okay stay warm, I'm coming." Stay warm when it's freezing out there, good one Helena. "You ready to go Grace?"

"Yep." She says while tying her shoelaces and then puts on her jacket, I help as she has trouble putting her arm through the sleeve.

"How much water you got?" I ask.

"Just what's in your water bottle, we didn't have time to get me one remember."

"Oh yes I remember now. Can you reach behind you anything we can use?"

Grace turns around and searches blindly in the pitch black.

"I've found something a box." She says and hands me a rectangle box.

Once I open it I find a rope and a flare gun, I pocket the flare gun just in case.

We climb out of the car and leave the cosy warmth behind.

Grace and I stand in the snow trying to listen to that stream, but I think it's frozen.

We did head over a bridge and then keep something that looked like a river to our left then we find another bridge and the keep the river to our right.

I start to hear it faintly, the streams force fighting to not freeze over.

The path is getting dangerous, I constantly check to make sure Grace is still safe.

We reach a gate where it's also fencing something off, when we step onto the snow we realize it's hiding train tracks underneath.

We head through the gate and continue on the path.

A lot of snow lands on my head from a tree branch. I shake it off and hear Grace laugh which makes me smile.

We stop and assess the path in front of us, it's a thin path single file only, with a drop into the frozen icy waters below.

There's even handles on the wall to cling to as you make your way on the path.

"We're going to tie this around ourselves." I say while retrieving the rope out of the bag.

I tie it around Graces waist and then around mine. I tug on it several times, it seems secure, I hope it is. I go first testing each part of the ledge before committing to the next step.

We reach halfway where the path begins to bend.

I hear Graces scream before the rope goes taught, I have seconds and cling tightly to the handles before the rope tries to pull me down with her.

The rope pulls hard around my waist.

"You good?" I shout when things go calm, hoping to hear her voice.

"Yes," she pauses. "Just a few bruises and cuts." I can hear the pain in her voice.

"Okay let's try get you back on the ledge." How I think to myself. "Okay can you climb?"

"Yes, but you'll need to pull on the rope, there's a rock above me."

Okay. Okay. I take one hand off the handle and feel for the rope behind me. I wrap it around my wrist and pull.

"Okay start to climb."

I can feel the rope begin to move as she begins to climb, until finally the rope loosens up and I can see her fingers gripping the ledges edge.

"Grab my hand." I say offering my hand that's got the rope still twisted around it.

I find extra strength and pull with my one hand while the other grips the handle.

Grace gets onto the ledge and hugs me so that she doesn't fall again.

I guide her hand to a handle.

"Are you alright?" I ask and I'm about to check her over.

"Can we please get off this ledge, then you can fuss over me."

We make it around the bend on the ledge and I immediately spot the cave.

Around the bend the path becomes stable again and we easily make our way to the cave without further incidents.

"Sergeant?" I shout into the cave.

"H-h-h-here." I hear, I reach him and shine the torch on him.

He's holding out matches in his frozen fingers. I retrieve some cotton out of my bag and manage to strike a match on the wall.

There's a howl coming from the cave entrance as the wind nearly blows the fire out, we protect it and Grace, and I sit next to the sergeant to try and keep some of the wind off him.

I don't even try to assess him until he can at least speak without chattering his teeth.

"Come here." I say softly to Grace whose face is bruised and cut.

She winced when I touch her ribs, her arms and legs have cuts, I clean them and bandage the worst ones.

Grace hugs me once I've finished, smiles, then sits back down next to the fire.

"You're my saviour." The sergeant says to me, laughing as he does.

"So, what happened to you?" I ask and nudge him to stop him laughing.

"We were hiking up a mountain, but a snow storm caught us unaware. It was completely white, that's when the first lost his footing and disappeared we couldn't go after him because we couldn't see. We decided to abandon the mission and head back. But it involved bumping into things on the way down. That's when I broke my foot and we lost a second and clearly the third as he isn't with you."

"Yes, he made it to the vehicle, but it seemed like he had bashed his head."

"I told him not to go, he said it was fine, he hadn't bashed his head that hard, he said that after a ledge we was on collapsed it threw one of us into the icy water and tossed the two of us near the water's edge."

"That happened to us, Grace got thrown off the ledge, but we had the rope." I say looking at Grace who is asleep next to the fire.

"We should head back soon while it's not snowing." He says.

"Can you walk?"

"No but we'll die here if we don't continue our journey south."

I nod in agreement and gently wake Grace up then try to help the sergeant stand but he screams in pain and sits down.

I try my best to wrap bandages around his broken leg and then wrap more bandages around his leg and a stick to give it some sort of support.

But I honestly don't know what I'm doing, I can't just do nothing.

He also winces as I wrap even more bandages around it.

"I know you're trying to help," he says through gritted teeth. "But anymore bandages and I think my leg will suffocate."

"Oh sorry." I say and finish up. "Any better?" I ask while helping him to his feet.

"Yes, I think we can make it slowly to the vehicle."

He is right we go slowly back. I make him go first on the ledge, so he can set the pace and I make Grace go second so I can keep an eye on her.

For extra safety, we all use the rope and tie it around ourselves.

We make it safely to the other side each time Grace puts a step forward I worry.

The way back is slow, we both help the sergeant who's starting to struggle and there's more snow on the path.

We make it to the vehicle, the sergeant stops at a mound of snow that's red. He knows it's his friend.

"Do you want me to bury him?" I ask.

"No." He says, "we're all exhausted let's get out of here. You're going to have to drive in case I pass out." He grabs my arm. "Honestly, thank you, you saved my life."

Grace takes the front passenger seat, so the sergeant can put his foot up.

I turn the car around and head the way we came. We checked the maps and it's the fastest way to a road that should take us to Cornwall.

16 FLARE

We stop in the night and sleep in the car, we go slower everyday as the snow continues to build on the empty roads.

We make it onto the motorway that will take us south, we make it a day on the motorway before we start to run low on petrol.

"Service station." Grace shouts as we're all looking for it, she's pointing to a restaurant sign.

We turn into it and see the petrol station.

Once I reach a pump I test it. Yep still works and I begin to fill the car up.

I put in what I think is enough and go to get back in the car when the sergeant stops me.

"Maybe we should go to the restaurant, over there?" He asks.

We do need food. "Okay but not you, you need rest, Grace you can come."

I grab my bag and make sure that my guns are loaded, then we go.

There's abandoned cars still in the car park, hopefully their occupants aren't inside.

We force the door open, it doesn't smell good, there's rotten food on the tables.

We jump the counter and then we're in the kitchen, no luck here.

Next thing I see is a pole coming towards me, I have no time to get out of the way.

I wake and immediately feel my hands tied behind back, then I panic and spot Grace to my left.

"Grace, I'm here, you'll be okay. I promise." I receive a punch to my face, but Grace seems to be calmer so it's worth it.

"Don't talk." The man says.

"How you get here?" Another asks.

They don't have guns but where's mine. I try shifting to feel mine and I do, they are there, they haven't searched me, good.

I receive a kick to the ribs for not answering.

"We walked here." I lie.

"So, you're alone?"

A horn goes off in the distance, I guess it's the sergeant.

"Go check it out." The man says to the other.

Good. I can take one as the handcuffs aren't too tight I started getting out of them when I woke.

The gunshots go off soon after, I get one hand free and reach for my weapon freezing my captive in his tracks.

I catch Grace's eye and realize I can't kill him in front of her she has been through enough.

The sergeant bursts in and is about to squeeze the trigger. "Don't." I shout.

"I'll leave." He begs.

"Go." I say and he runs past the sergeant out of the door.

"Why did you let him go?" The sergeant asks sounding annoyed.

"Because we shouldn't kill him."

"Well we can't stay here, he'll be back with more people and it's getting dark."

"Then we'll sleep in the vehicle on the road somewhere."

The sergeant leaves and I help Grace out of the handcuffs and remove my own.

We fill up a jerry can before leaving.

We drive for what feels like an hour and I'm losing focus when driving so I stop the vehicle turn off all lights and sleep.

Grace puts her legs on me so that she can fully lie down and hopefully have a good night's rest.

A few days pass before we must use the jerry can to fill up the vehicle up.

The sergeant says we are nearing Cornwall but how do I know. I mean how does he know there's been road signs, but they've been covered in snow and we haven't stopped to look.

"The fuel gauge is getting low." I say to the sergeant as an indicator appeared.

"Well we're not risking another gas station, we will use what's left, then walk."

I don't object, I think it's safer to not visit the petrol stations.

"Who wants the last biscuit?" Grace asks.

"You can have it." I say and the sergeant doesn't object. I would have fought him if he did.

Just off the tiny bit of petrol in the tank we get a few days before the vehicle starts to slow down to a complete stop.

"I think we ran out of petrol." I say after trying and failing several times to start the car.

"Looks like we're walking." The sergeant says and begins to gather his things.

We step out of the warm car and once again into the freezing cold, we all take one look back and walk into the snow.

We're following the road that takes us south but after a few weeks walking the sergeant re-checks his maps.

"This road," he says pointing to it on the map, "is the one we are on, we need to cut across these fields and then we'll hit the Cornwall borders."

"But it will take ages with your leg." I say as we've been helping him all this way.

"We have no choice." He says and I know, none of us have eaten for a few days and Grace and I only have the one water bottle between us. When we try to sleep in the tent you can hear the grumble of our stomachs.

A few days we are walking when Grace and I stop supporting the sergeant when walking, it's the sergeant's decision we are all too tired and slowly starving.

We do make him stronger walking sticks which seems to be working better than having two sleepy starved people to support him.

We are just in front of him, finding the best route when I feel Grace's hand touch mine, she must be scared I am as well if I am honest, we don't know if anyone is out here and we are starving to death. We need to find some people.

I hold onto her hand as we battle the wind, good job my hair is tied back so it's out of my face, Grace though is fighting a battle with her hair.

We stop, I tie her hair up and she smiles to thank me and grabs my hand again, we then continue against the elements.

The sergeant tells us not to stop for him as we might not get started again plus there is a storm that's coming from behind us.

I look behind again and can see the storm, the sky looks so angry, a storm for sure.

Ugh, great a hill and I'm so tired we are all going to pass out but that storms coming we need to continue.

My legs are moving forward for the sake of moving forward, I can't even feel my legs they've went numb either with the cold or with the lack of food.

Grace's arm is slowly being dragged by me as I can feel her losing energy, I'm more helping her up the hill than her walking with me.

Just before I reach the top of the hill I hear it first a thud in the snow behind me.

I look behind and the sergeant is no longer there, most likely past out and is lying in the snow.

I need to first evaluate what's over the hill then quickly go back for him.

But I can feel my own eye lids trying to close.

I reach the top of the hill but can't go any further as Grace won't allow me, I turn around and find her also passed out.

My eyesight is also going, but can I see... I fumble around in my pocket remembering the flare gun.

I take it out before falling into the snow myself and losing grip on Graces hand.

I use my remaining energy to lift my arm and squeeze the trigger sending the flare into the sky.

My eyes close for a second before re-opening and I can see the search light coming.

I close my eyes for a few minutes and can see the helicopter. I close my eyes to shield them from the snow being flicked up by the blades.

I try to open my eyes again, but I can't, and I feel myself slowly drifting off.

17 GENERAL

When I wake I have no clue where I am, it feels like there is warmth at least, although I don't feel all the weight of my layers of clothing.

I'm on my back looking up at the roof, a green canvas roof.

I turn my head to the left, there's a nurse checking my clip board.

"Who..." I try to ask but my voice is hoarse.

"Ah, you're awake. Who changed your clothes a female nurse, they were filthy..."

"I don't care about that." I cut her off. "I meant where's Grace?"

"Who?"

"Grace." She's starting to annoy me, I go to stand but my hands are handcuffed to the bed.

I begin to rattle the bed trying to brake it, I need to find Grace.

"Calm down." The nurse says, then shouts, "guard."

A guard comes in wearing military gear and holding what looks like a military rifle.

"Do you want me to ask the guard to knock you out with his gun? We don't have any sedatives."

"No." I say and calm down, I can't find Grace if I am not conscious. "Why am I handcuffed? And where's Grace, I need to see her."

"Look." The nurse says. "You're in a field hospital you are also a prisoner because you had weapons which if I am correct come with a prison sentence." The nurse turns to the guard. "Was she brought in with anyone?"

"Yes, a girl and a sergeant."

"Yes, the girl." I say, "she's my sister, her names Grace, can I see her?"

"No." The guard answers. "You're a prisoner the sergeant vouches for you but only someone high up can grant you immunity."

Think, Think. I wrote the security firms number down, maybe they

81

could help.

"Look, I can clear this up. Can I have my bag?" I ask.

The guard and the nurse look at each other, the nurse pulls out a bunch of keys and walks to a locker and retrieves my bag, the nurse places it on my bed.

"Can you un-cuff one of my hands please?" The guard looks at me like there's not a chance. "You can point the gun at me, please I need one hand at least."

He does point the gun at me while the nurse un-cuffs my hand, I pull out all the contents except the money. I'll bribe him if all else fails.

Here it is, the piece of paper. "Here call that number, my name is Helena, I work for them." I hope this works.

The nurse cuffs my hand then the guard lowers his gun and takes the paper and jogs away.

The nurse leaves to check on her other patients when she comes to check on me I ask how long he's been and she says an hour, but it feels like twenty hours.

Then I see him, well he's behind someone who looks in charge. He's holding a satellite phone.

The man clearly in charge stands at the end of my bed and salutes me while the guard begins to quickly un-cuff both my hands.

"Sorry ma'am." The man says. "We didn't know. I'm Lieutenant George, there's a phone call for you."

"Hello." I say when he hands me the phone and I am relieved that it worked.

"You need to act like a general." It's a woman's voice on the other end.

"A what?" I say, and the lieutenant looks at me strangely.

"If they are still there say yes, put on a serious face."

"Yes." I say with a scowl on my face.

"Well I work for BPB, well for now I work for that security company. The one you have to work for to pay off your crimes."

"I remember." I say, how can I not.

"Well," she says. "I didn't have much time to get you out of this mess, but I made some calls, who then made some calls. Anyway, there were some chatter of your grandparent the one that died recently and the calls came back with results."

"Simplified version please." I say as I need to find Grace.

"Well you are now an official General of a secret splinter army that works with, secretly of course, the public army."

I have many questions, but all would be suspicious in front of this Lieutenant, the woman on the phone senses it.

"Okay." She says on the phone. "So, I know you have a lot of questions as do I. I will contact you at your home address for an interview when the storms over. For now, you must act like a General. You are the bases superior commander, I'm sure you've watched some movies make it up, just don't go over the top."

"Are we on a secure connection?" I ask, I might as well do as she says even though I have no clue of what's going on, how can a normal person become a high-ranking officer of some secret military that I know nothing about.

"Good, you're getting the hang of it. I have to go."

I end the call, well luckily, she ends it as I couldn't find the button.

"Do you have spare clothes Lieutenant?" I ask trying to put on a commanding voice or am I just shouting.

The Lieutenant clicks his fingers trying to show off because he thinks I am a General, the soldier next to him hands him a pile of folded clothes. Military uniform.

"I'll be outside." The Lieutenant says.

The nurse closes the curtains around my bed, I change into the military green uniform and roll up the edges as they are a little too big. I also put on the green cap that's supplied.

I catch myself in the small mirror on the bed side table, this uniform suits me. I notice my slouched shoulders and stand tall and back straight as I am a General now. I laugh at the thought a General has someone lost their mind, or have I.

I fasten my military boots which are my size, they are very shiny.

I leave the bed area and find the nurse.

"Where is Grace?" I ask her.

"The Lieutenant will show you."

I open the tent flap, it's not snowing but it's cold and there is snow on the floor.

"Can you take me to my sister please?" Was that to polite should I have demanded it.

"Sure, this way ma'am."

"Call me Helena." I say then look at his hands. "And what's that?" He's holding some sort of badge.

"Oh yes, it's your insignia, Private." He shouts to a soldier behind us. "Get my sewing kit."

"Mine?" I ask.

"Yes, you need the insignia on you, I don't want a soldier being disciplined for disobeying a General's orders."

"Fine but we are not stopping you can sew it on my shoulder when we are at Graces bedside."

We enter the tent and I spot her immediately and walk faster towards her trying not to run.

"What's wrong?" I ask Grace as she looks white as a ghost, she tries to talk but begins to cough. "Don't talk save your energy."

The Lieutenant goes to find a nurse, Grace points behind me, it's the soldier saluting me.

"I'll explain later." I whisper to Grace. "At ease soldier." I say to the soldier, I remember someone saying it on a film but maybe at ease would have been enough.

The soldier stops saluting. "Ma'am where's the Lieutenant? I have his things."

"Here he is." He's coming back with a nurse.

The nurse picks up Grace's clipboard at the end of her bed. "So, you're her sister?"

"Yes." Small talk while he looks through the notes.

"Well Grace here has a nasty virus."

"Don't you have anti-biotics?"

"No, our supply vehicle got stuck in the snow and we are all out. There are rumours of a local pharmacy charging a ridiculous amount of money for them and the military as you know have been advised not to take them by force." He shakes his head.

"But how did this happen to Grace the last time I was with her she was fine."

"We found a wound on her leg which was infected."

I failed her, I checked her in that cave to make sure nothing was infected. "Can you write down the anti-biotic that she needs." The nurse does. "Thanks." I say and the nurse leaves.

"Can I?" The Lieutenant asks holding the needle, thread and a General insignia.

"Sure." He puts his hand under my sleeve and begins to sew. "Soldier can you bring me a vehicle and my weapons."

"Ah." I shout to the Lieutenant after a few minutes silence as the needle hits and breaks my skin.

"Sorry." He says. "Don't normally sew while a person's wearing the piece of clothing." He carries on more carefully. "All done."

I look at it, it's a General badge. Well I'm not a military person so I take his word that it is.

The soldier comes back with a solid looking case.

"Here and here ma'am." He says holding the case and the keys out.

The solider drops the keys into my open palm and hands me the case.

I un-clip the case and find my guns and holsters inside and an extra holster for the silencers.

I set the holsters up and I am relieved to feel the guns under both arms. I feel a little more protected.

Grace waves her hand in the air I don't know what she wants.

"Bracelet." Grace says through a croaky voice as I lean in to hear.

"I said I'd be back for it, but I'm here for you, besides anyway I told you, you can keep it."

She shakes her hand, then my thoughts click it's not on her wrist.

"Where's her things?" I ask the lieutenant.

He leaves, then comes back with a key then takes me to a locker.

There's her clothes, the pink sweater which is technically mine but there's no personal things. Like her bag or her phone which she usually looks at a picture of her parents and the bracelet is gone.

"Lieutenant who has access to this?"

"Mainly military personnel, then the keys are given to the nurses in case a bed can be freed up. Why?"

"My sisters missing a few things."

"Are you sure?" He asks, I don't have time to answer he quickly adds, "sorry ma'am what is missing?"

"A phone, bracelet, her bag is missing as well. The phone has like a bunny rabbit ears on the case."

"I'll find it Helena and whoever has taken it will be disciplined."

I nod at him and he salutes then leaves.

"Grace I'll be back soon, I need to get you medicine." I kiss her on the forehead and leave.

I get to the car where a soldier salutes me.

"Ma'am," he's young compared to the other soldiers I've seen, "the Lieutenant told me to go with you."

"Get in then." He climbs in the back, I find my bag on the seat and move it over to the passenger seat.

I put my cap on the seat and drive, the private in the back tells me the way to go.

Once I reach the gate I'm stopped by a guard. "Ma'am." He salutes. "You might need a coat."

I root through my bag and find my jacket it's not very military looking but it's comfy.

"Let her through." He shouts, and the barrier is raised.

The roads clear but eventually there's snow and the added snowplough makes easy work of moving it.

We make it to the pharmacy, I tell the private to wait in the car and I take my bag with me.

Ding, a bell goes off above my head as I open the door to the pharmacy.

"I've told the military I will not be handing over my supplies" A woman behind the counter says.

"I'm here on personal business."

"Oh." The pharmacist says now standing still with an intrigued expression.

I place the piece of paper on the counter. "Do you have this anti-biotic?"

The person retrieves their glasses out of a top pocket and reads, then heads to the back out of view.

The pharmacist places it on the counter, I read the label and yup that's it.

"How much?"

"How much you offering?" She asks.

"Two thousand." They're going to charge me way over sticker price anyway, I'm not going to ten thousand and then she says eleven.

"Three thousand."

"Five thousand and you give me an extra bottle and a half."

"Deal." They say after thinking about it. They leave, and I quickly get the money out and place it on the counter.

"You might as well take the three, it's all I've got left and I won't be able to sell half."

"Thanks." I force myself to say as I don't want to as she is killing people, but I may be back if I need more medicine.

I climb back into the vehicle and head back.

The nurse bumps into me on the way to Grace.

"Is this what you need?" I ask him.

"Yes, I can give it to her now, meet me there I'll get my things."

"Wait I've got these extra two for anyone that needs it immediately."

"This will help a lot." He takes the two and heads off.

The nurse comes back with another nurse whose holding various medical equipment.

A needle is one of them it punctures and then I can't look in case they put it into her arm, I hate needles.

"Is that it, will she get better?"

"Yes, she should start getting better over the next few days if not then another dose should do it."

Before they leave they write more information on the clipboard.

I fall asleep and wake when I feel Graces hand slipping into mine, I give it a gentle squeeze.

"How are you feeling?"

"A little better." She says.

At least she can talk now, we talk a little while longer before she rests and as per her instructions I brush her hair.

18 MESSENGER

The lieutenant wakes me and salutes. "Helena, I found your sisters things." He swings a bag off his back. I take the bag and first pick up the phone. "I also charged that. I found a charger that fitted, it's in the bag."

"Thanks where did you find her things?"

"In a soldier's locker, he stole quite a lot. The military police have him, he'll be going to prison."

I nod to him as it sounds like a fitting punishment. "Also, where's the sergeant the one I came in with?"

"He's recovering. The Private I've assigned you will be able to tell you where he is."

"Thanks."

The Lieutenant salutes then he leaves.

Grace begins to recover quickly, she's able to walk about now and allows me to wash her hair.

Eventually the nurse says that she is okay to leave which is good news as the drip can now come out.

I've been meaning to see the sergeant, but I didn't want to leave Graces bedside. So, with Graces new freedom we decide to go there first.

The sergeant is also in a field hospital military personnel only but of course we're allowed in.

He looks healthier and he salutes me, so word must have travelled.

"You good?" I ask.

"Yeah, getting better broke a few bones though. How come you didn't tell me you're a General?"

He's straight to the point, gotta lie quickly. "You know I'm from a splinter army, I came from a mission to get information from an asset. I was with my sister, so I wasn't going to risk exposing myself as a General."

He's suspicious, ugh. "How come you acted like you couldn't drive."

"I thought it'd be in character you'd be less suspicious of me."

"Sorry ma'am." He says and salutes me again.

"Well I hope you make a speedy recovery." I say and quickly leave. I'm not that cold-hearted leaving this quickly but he is clearly very suspicious.

I told Grace while she was getting better about what had happened. I had to tell her when we went for walks careful to make sure no one could listen.

She said it was strange, which I agreed.

I also told the Lieutenant to keep himself in charge of the compound and Grace and I have accommodation in our private tent, but we've also asked the Lieutenant to find us better accommodation.

He does within a day a static caravan on one of the local farms.

I take it, but he assigns us another guard, a female higher ranking than the other. She looks more experienced than the other.

It's starting to rain more now which is a better sign than snow but it's making the roads icy.

Our caravan is big, but Grace still chooses to sleep on the king-sized bed with me.

With Grace's help I put a few maps and random words on paper on the table so if anyone visits then I look like I'm doing something.

On one-day Grace makes me feel guilty, it's raining and she tells me it's mean that the two soldiers are sat outside.

So, I ask them to come inside but they have to make things difficult by saying they can't because they have orders. Ugh, Grace still expects me to do something.

"One can sit in the vehicle." I say chucking the keys at them, "and the other can come inside."

They agree, and the female soldier comes inside.

Grace looks happy which means I'm now happy, but I am also running around hiding papers.

I wake one morning next to Grace, and I can hear the faint noise of a vehicle.

I head to the far end of the caravan and pull back the curtain to find a car, military driving fast down the lane its snowplough not even needing to be used as it hasn't snowed in a few days.

My guards stop the vehicle and salute to whoever is inside, I stop peering out the window in case they see me.

I change out of my dressing gown in the spare room to my military gear. I can hear them knocking.

"Coming." I shout and straighten my collar.

I open the door to find the Lieutenant and what looks like a messenger.

"Come in, sit." I say showing them to the couch which you can't really miss in a caravan. "Tea?"

"Yes, please two sugars." The Lieutenant says.

"No thanks." The messenger replies.

I make tea and sit down on a chair opposite; the messenger places a leather bag on the table.

"From your superiors." He says.

Can you even have superiors when you're a General?

I find a wax seal which has a cross of some sort on it.

The contents tip into my lap, I don't know how the contents even fitted into the envelope.

There's ink, a quill, a ring with a large face which has the same cross engraved into it and a hand-written letter which is rare, usually they are just typed up on a computer.

The letter reads:

To General Helena Orban.

Your uncle who recently passed has done many contracts for our cause. We are an organization that takes pride in our secrecy. As stated above we have always used the Orban family when we needed a matter taken care of, but for you we extend our hand, we want you to be a part of our organization. From the ring you received which you must wear always, you may be able to guess the name of our organization, but we have changed since then, we no longer believe in religion but until now we have never had a high-ranking female. If you accept your role leave the caravan light on in the kitchen and write a simple accept in an envelope which should be wax sealed using the ring and a candle which is in the bag.

Regards

The Grand Master.

P.S Burn this letter or we will know and have no choice but to burn the caravan down. Do it NOW.

I panic a little as the last part sends shivers down my spine.

"Do you have a lighter?" I ask the lieutenant calmly.

He hands me one, I light the corner and watch it burn then drop it into the ash tray and watch it turn to ashes.

"Sensitive information." I say to the Lieutenant who's trying not to look at me as strangely as he is.

I can't gather my thoughts as they are watching me, and I must decide.

First things first deal with these two, but then I spot something.

The messengers wearing a similar ring much smaller and cheaper looking but I decide not to confront him.

"So, Lieutenant you have information?" I ask.

"Ah yes," he slides a brown envelope across the table. "It's all in there, we've managed to get a supply truck in, a small one mainly carrying medical supplies anti-biotics like you asked. A month max and we'll be able to head back to the barracks."

I look inside the envelope there's satellite images of the area, one has a lot of snow one doesn't.

"Is that all?" I ask but maybe that wasn't kind of me.

"Yes." He stands and salutes.

"Wait." I catch him before he leaves making sure the messenger is outside. "Do you know this insignia?" I ask holding up the ring normally I'd use the internet.

"Yes, it's a knights templar ring."

"Thanks, and if you can tomorrow night a late dinner at eight when the base should be quiet, you, me and Grace?"

"Yes ma'am, I'll be there." He says and leaves.

Grace is now awake, awake but still in bed.

"Who was it?" She asks while rubbing her eyes, I tell her but leave out the letter that's my decision.

"Oh, and you told me to be more sociable, so the Lieutenant is coming to eat tomorrow night."

I hear her sigh.

The rest of the day and night we eat snacks under a blanket on the couch and watch films that we found in a cabinet.

19 FOOD

We wake early with a plan to get some ingredients and a cook book as I'm not the best cook and to get Grace some new clothes.

The weather is blue skies and sunshine but it's still cold out and yes, I decided to take the job with that private military otherwise who knows, they are watching me and could easily kill Grace and me.

I ask the guards if they saw anything as the notes been taken off the door, yup they sleep in the car. But they say they haven't saw anything.

We wait in the car while they use the bathroom to freshen up.

We head into the village, I make the guards mind the car after some arguing they realize that it's for the best as I have guns and I'm wearing a civilian jacket.

We head to a clothes store we've been told it's the only one or rather the only one that's opened they also sell food but apparently, they are now charging too much for items.

We walk in and yep overpriced, un-named clothes for treble of what they are worth, but Grace has caught her eye on something.

A wintry grey jumper with light grey sleeves with some sort of pattern on it.

"Can I get it?" She asks, I can't say no even though its two hundred pounds.

We continue looking, I also buy a pair of jeans that have an intended rip at the knee. I must admit she has an eye for style I need to remember to take her with me to go shopping.

I also buy her an extra pair of pyjamas and a pair for myself the only reasonably priced thing in here.

We both spot a pair of joggers and they are super soft, we have to buy them no one can really relax in a pair of jeans, I end up paying one thousand for Grace's and mine but it's worth it.

We head next to a grocery store that is apparently cheaper than here, again they are expensive but less than the clothes store. There is even a sign that reads essential items that seem to be close to normal prices.

I buy what I think I need, I'm making homemade burgers well made by me in not my home, everybody loves burgers.

When I turn around and Grace is gone, I find her in a different isle, spreadable isle.

She's holding something as if she had just found gold.

"Can I have it?" She asks as I near her. "I wouldn't ask because of the price but my mum used to buy me it." She adds with a quiet, sadder sort of tone.

"Sure." I say, as it can cost whatever, and I'd still buy it to make her happy.

I take the peanut butter off her and place it in the basket.

It still comes to a large sum; the peanut butter was half the cost of all the items put together.

We get back to the caravan. Grace puts her feet up while reading a book while I put the shopping away.

I pop in some bread in the toaster while I do.

I make Grace and me peanut butter on toast, she looks excited when I bring it to her.

Grace snuggles into me when I sit next to her.

Once the toast is finished I go to start on the burgers, I make enough for the two soldiers who are sitting in the car.

I go to join Grace on the couch and read. The sky out of the caravan window looks fascinating the blue sky with a faint pink colour.

A knock on the door makes me realize the time.

Lieutenant George stands on the steps.

"I don't know what to bring." He says holding out a bag.

I take the bag and look inside there's wine, whiskey, cider, beer and a chocolate cake.

"You covered everything." I say, and he laughs. "Come in, come in."

"Hello Grace, glad you are looking well." He says to her.

"Thanks." Grace says and continues to read.

I move my book, so he can sit. "TV remote is there, or you can sit at the dining table and talk to me while I cook."

"I'll sit at the dining table then." He says, I feel awkward, I've never had to entertain a guest before.

We talk a while then the burgers are done, he chooses a beer and I choose a cider.

I send Grace out with two plates with burgers and chips for the soldiers.

We wait for Grace to come back then eat.

"It's not my place," the Lieutenant starts the conversation. "But I've met one General in my career and they never treat their guards or people of a lower rank, like you did."

I think it's a compliment with a hint of suspicion.

I take a bite from my burger then answer. "Well," I have nothing. "There's two reasons or more than two, our private military have their own soldiers of course, so I am making sure your soldiers like me even just a little. If or when the times comes and if we are ever outnumbered, they'll fight beside me. Or it could even be only because you've only ever met one."

"Yes, maybe other Generals are different."

We talk and eat more, I make sure the conversation stays on him.

It does, and I start to learn more about him, he has a wife and two kids who are waiting out this freak storm in their basement, with enough firewood for their log burner and enough food to last them a lifetime.

He's also constantly in contact with them through a satellite phone.

We eat desert, the chocolate cake that's delicious, I don't even know how he managed to get it.

"The bakery has just open up, prices are alright." He says before I could ask, his words are a little slurred.

There's no conversation and I'm worried he'll ask something about me.

"So, when is the army moving out?"

"Well, orders are next week. Roads are clearing quickly every vehicle with a snowplough is being sent onto the motorway. I have a squad using one of the Humvees on the motorway now."

"The roads are clear then?"

"Yep, well motorways in a few days, yes."

"We can go home then?" I ask.

"Yep, well you'll need to finish your business here, your commanders want you to do something and you'll need to see me to officially sign off base."

"What do they want me to do?"

"I can't remember, you'll have to see me in the morning." He goes to stand but stumbles and grabs the back of my chair to steady himself.

He's had a lot more to drink but not here. Something must be troubling him.

"Are you heading back to base?" I ask as he's unsure where he's going.

"Yes ma'am." He salutes as he opens the door and nearly falls down the caravan steps.

I help him down the last few steps and get one of the guards to drive him back to base and stay there until morning.

The other soldier agrees to sleep on the couch she insists that she must be close enough to guard on her own.

20 PACKAGE

I wake to find Grace for once already awake as she isn't on the bed.

"There's a bowl of cereal on the table." Grace says.

"Thanks." I say and take the bowl, I kiss her on the head and sit next to her.

I quickly eat then get dressed.

"Grab your coat we're going to see the Lieutenant." I didn't want to take Grace on business, but I still feel like we are being watched. She's safer with me.

We reach the army base where everyone is still saluting me I don't think it will ever feel normal.

I pull up outside the command tent, once inside I find the Lieutenant behind a desk.

"Ah Helena, good to see you." I left Grace in the car as she's safe here. "Here are your instructions."

I read them, they want me to pick up a package and leave it in the vehicle outside my house which is miles away.

"So, you said it's okay to head home?" I ask.

"Yes, the motorways are clear they may be very icy though."

"Then I'll be heading home today but I'll need to be keeping the vehicle."

"Okay I've been told to take the guards off you." He says and stands. "Good luck."

I shake his hand and leave.

The two soldiers that have been guarding me salute and leave.

I sit in the car relieved.

"What's going on?" Grace asks.

"We're going home."

"Now?"

"No, I've got to pick something up, then pick our things up from the caravan, then yes."

"It would be good to see where you live." She takes my phone out of her pocket. "Can we take a selfie?"

"Here? Right now?"

She nods.

"Fine." I say and fix my hair in the mirror.

Grace quickly takes it and she seems happy. She's took several pictures of us two I think she wants memories of the two of us.

We exit the base hopefully for the last time.

We head to the address which is further into the countryside, then begin to drive up a long driveway with huge statues either side.

The huge statues are dwarfed by the large house with its many windows.

A man stands at the doorway ready to greet us.

Grace winds the windows down so I can ask him if I'm in the right place.

"You are the General?" He asks.

"I am."

"Come in, my master gave me orders not to touch it."

He takes me to a large room with a table in the centre, on the table a chest.

"Before I give you the key can I see your hand?"

Which hand? But I guess the one with the templar ring on.

I was right he hands me a key inside is a few letters and a parcel. I take them and leave.

Grace takes my hand as we leave. Yep she came with me, I wasn't going to leave her in the car.

"Do you know what it is?" Grace asks as we climb into the car.

"No, I don't want to find out either."

I start the car and speed off. We get into the village before I realise a car has been following us for a while.

I speed up and the car behind does the same.

"Why are we speeding?" Grace asks sounding worried.

"I think we're being followed."

Grace looks back, which is a bad idea as they now know that I know they're there.

They speed up and ram my car.

I look at Grace and I am glad she has her seat belt on.

I begin to weave in and out of the little traffic, but they are still following.

They keep trying to drive next to me but there's no space.

But we are heading out of town quickly at least I'll be able to shoot once we are out of town.

"Get in the footwell." I say to Grace, she does as I say, with a scared look on her face.

The car behind speeds up, then begins to overtake, I quickly lower the window and take out my gun.

I can see them now, two of them, both wearing masks.

The driver leans back, and his passenger takes out a gun.

I begin to fire into their car, I'm trying to focus on driving and shooting. So, when their car screeches and begins to fall back I don't know if I shot anyone.

I wind the window up and speed up, I'm not going to hang around.

"You can take your seat now."

Grace sits, but she's quiet I don't know if she's scared of me or angry with me.

We head straight for the caravan.

We pull up outside. "Grace, I need you to get everything of ours and put it in the car while I keep a look out."

She nods and runs up the steps into the caravan, she brings out our rucksacks first with our things stuffed inside.

The second time she's got her arms full of food and throws it on the back seat.

"All done?" I ask.

Grace nods and climbs in the car.

She's still silent, like when we met at that clearing. I try to make small talk but nothing.

After driving on the motorway which is clear of snow, but there's still icy patches here and there, we pull over.

I look on the back seat for food only bread and...

I chuck the peanut butter to Grace. Her eyes go wide like I've just gave her gold.

"Eat up might as well eat it all."

"But I don't have a spoon."

"Use your fingers." She looks at me like, can I? "Go on."

The second time I tell her she gives in and uses her fingers to scoop it out.

I use some of my water to wash her hands while she asks, "How long will it take to get to your home?"

"Our home now, should be home by tea time."

I drive fast but sensible, sometimes there is still snow but the plough does its job.

21 HOME

It's still light when we reach the outskirts of Liverpool, we head further in and come across a checkpoint.

We can see the liver birds in the distance.

A soldier waves us in so we stop.

He shines a torch into the car and instantly stops and salutes, I guess he salutes because of the insignia on my top.

"Sorry ma'am we weren't told."

"It's alright can you let us through?"

He stops saluting and looks uneasy. "Sorry ma'am, can't do that have to ask my superior. Going to have to ask you for your keys."

Annoying but he's just doing his job. I pass him the keys and he heads off to a hut.

An officer heads towards us.

"So, you're a General, I'm going to need to see your driving license."

The only thing I don't have. "I don't have it, I lost it."

"Convenient I radioed command and there is no General in the area."

"Can I get something from my bag?"

He motions for me to do so. I pull out the card with the number on.

He heads back to his hut, eventually he comes back out and salutes.

"Sorry ma'am, had to be careful. Here's some leaflets we have to give out to people going home which I'm sure you are?"

"Yep." He hands us several leaflets.

"Will you be needing an escort?"

"Nope."

"Let them through." He says and gives a final salute.

"What to do if your home door is open." Grace says as she reads through the leaflets.

She places one in my lap.

"What is it?" I ask as I am trying to drive.

"Adoption."

"Oh." She places another in my lap. "What's this one?"

"Food."

"Well here we are." I say and stop the car outside the house.

Grace looks out the window. "It looks big."

"Well it's quite small inside. Here's the keys, I'll grab the bags."

Grace takes the keys and heads slowly towards the house.

She's standing in the open doorway. "Go on." I say nudging her into the house and she starts in the living room, then into the kitchen.

"It's nice, it feels cosy." She says while having a look in the cupboards.

I drop the bags on the couch.

"Come on, I'll show you upstairs."

We reach the landing when she asks why is there a bullet hole in the door, he fixed everything except that.

"That's a long story, your room is here." We head to the spare room, the beds a mess from when I slept in it, ugh.

"I'll have to find new bedding."

"Who slept in it?"

"Me, when I was being lazy and didn't want to change the sheets on my own bed." She laughs. "I'll also have to buy you a wardrobe and a desk."

Next, we head to my room.

"Cool." She says and runs to the bookshelf that wraps around the rooms walls interrupted only by the fire.

"I haven't had time to look at them yet, you're welcome to read them just show me before you do, so I know it's appropriate."

Grace nods in agreement and goes to the nearest shelf.

I leave her in my room and go to check on the package.

It's left in the car like I was asked, with the doors not locked.

Everything of ours I take out. Once done I look up and down the street who knows are they watching me.

Heading back in I search the cupboard for food only crackers that are still in date.

I find the leaflet about food, they have one supermarket open but only between nine a.m. and eleven a.m. and it's way past that.

They also have pizza delivery but only on a Saturday and it's Friday ugh. I know I'm an adult and I'm meant to be looking after Grace, but it looks like we are eating crackers.

I've also picked up the adoption leaflet. I thought it was quite an odd topic for a leaflet but apparently there is a lot of children that need homes.

The first page reads once you are home if you are in the presence of a displaced child attend the nearest community centre ASAP (open 9-4 everyday).

There's not much information on the procedure, hmm.

I take the crackers and go to find Grace.

Grace is still in my room looking at books, so I take a seat in the chair as the beds a mess.

"Grace, we have two things to discuss."

She comes over with a book in hand. "Can I read this?"

Grace hands me the book, I read the blurb and it seems fine, so I nod and hand it back.

It's the first time I notice her clothes are filthy, well my jumper.

"First," I say. "There's a bag under my bed with my clothes inside, take it and get changed into something clean. Might be a little big but my sweater seems to fit you fine." As we didn't have a washing machine in the caravan I suspect the clothes we bought in Cornwall are also dirty.

Grace climbs under the bed and retrieves my bag. "Thanks." She says before leaving to change.

When Grace comes back she drops the bag on the bed then stands in front of me and does a spin in my pink pyjamas, which makes us both laugh.

Once she picks up her book she takes a seat on my lap clearly not realizing that's she's not a small child and my legs start to fall asleep, but I leave her be and stroke her hair.

"What did you want to talk to me about?" Grace asks.

"Oh, we only have crackers to eat, here." She takes one. "Shops aren't open until tomorrow and I have to ask again do you want me to adopt you?"

She shifts in my lap and looks at me with a serious expression. "Of course, I wouldn't want anyone else looking out for me. I think you'd do a good job at raising me."

It fills my heart with warmth to hear such things. "Okay, well it has to happen tomorrow first thing, the leaflet is telling people to do it ASAP."

She smiles and says, "Okay." Then continues to read her book.

I pick up my book from the table next to me, I read it while stroking her hair.

22 ADOPTION

I wake the next day to find blankets have been placed over me and I can't feel my legs.

When I stand I steady myself and get the blood flowing back in them again.

"Grace." I shout. I hear her downstairs.

"I washed my hair, but I didn't get a shower because I don't have clothes and there's no electricity so my heads cold." Grace says quickly as if she been waiting to tell me.

"Here." I get my cap which is on the couch and place it on her head. "What time is it?"

Grace hands me my phone. "It's eight, I was using your phone to play games on, hope you don't mind."

"Of course, I don't." I can tell it hurts slightly when she turns her phone on as she has pictures of her and her parents together. "Go change into some of my clothes, then we'll head to the adoption centre."

Grace comes back down wearing my jeans and a t-shirt and my cap. She is starting to look like a mini version of me, what cute monster have I created.

Grace hands me my pyjamas neatly folded. "I didn't know where to put them she adds."

I take them and place them on the couch. "You might need them tonight if the shop doesn't have anything."

I head upstairs and stand in front of my clothes, what am I going to wear.

I choose jeans and a t-shirt, but I throw my shirt over it, the one with the general insignia. It might help me at this adoption place and I'm nervous.

Grace has my cap, but I find a spare as my hair is a mess.

100

I hide my guns under the bed, I don't want to get myself into a mess again.

Paperwork hmm, I find my birth certificate hidden in my bag, I am also taking that card with that number for BPB.

That's all the paperwork I own. Once back down the stairs Grace is waiting.

"Let's go then."

Once outside I quickly notice the car is still there.

"Wait here." I approach the car cautiously.

The package has gone and there's a note on the seat it reads: 'You may need a car, we'll take it back when you receive one from BPB. Keys are in the ignition.'

Well that's not creepy, but hey looks like I've got a mode of transport.

"Come on." I say to Grace and open the door for her.

I've been to the community centre and it isn't that far and we're early so there shouldn't be that many people.

We turn the corner and nope, there's a long line of adults and kids.

I press hard on the accelerator and stop immediately where there's soldiers, they'll recognize the military vehicle. I hope.

One sticks his head in the open window the rest draw their weapons.

Then they immediately recognize the insignia and salute.

I step out the car and walk onto the pavement.

"At ease." They stop saluting.

"We weren't told you were in the area."

"I'm from a splinter army."

"Well I must get my superior ma'am."

He leaves and comes back with an older man who has a thick moustache on his upper lip.

He also salutes. "What's ye business here ma'am?"

The people in the que to our left are starting to get impatient.

"I'm here to adopt Grace." I say motioning to Grace.

"Well you'll have to go through processing and then we'll have to verify who you work with. This way."

We head inside.

"Adults that way." He points to one corridor. "Children that way." He points to another corridor.

"Is that necessary?"

"Yes, you have to be interviewed separately."

"I'll see you in a minute." I say to Grace. I should have brought my weapons.

They take me into a room, a woman enters a few minutes later clutching a notepad.

She puts a tape into the machine and presses start.

"Tape one, interviewer: Cat. Interviewing, state your name."

"Helena." She's writing it down as we speak, she isn't even looking at me, rude.

"Occupation?"

"General for a splinter army and BPB agent." I think it's an agent. If I say it with confidence hopefully she won't check as I haven't even had an induction yet.

"When was your first contact with," she flicks a page, "Grace?"

I explain how I met her and the circumstances.

"Her parents are deceased then?"

"Yes."

"And the location?"

The rough location I tell her as I don't know specifics.

"We only ask the location in case the police find a body, this way it's in the database and then they don't waste time trying to find who murdered them." She explains. "Do you have proof of who you are?"

I hand over my birth certificate I don't have any photographic ID.

"And one last thing proof of occupation?"

Damn it. "I've only got this card, you'll have to call the number." I say and hand it over.

"I'll be right back." She says and takes her notepad and my documents with her.

I notice there's a soldier standing on the other side of the door.

It's annoying sitting here, I want to get back to Grace.

The door opens slowly, and I see Grace running at me with a smile on her face.

Grace jumps on me and hugs me hard almost causing me to lose my breath.

Grace takes hold of my hand tightly as we head out of the door.

"This way." Cat the administrator says, we follow her through a corridor then into a large hall which has several desks at the far end.

"Sit, sit." She says and takes a seat opposite. "Sorry about the whole procedure, of course it's not usually conducted in this manner there's home visits, suitability checks etc. but this place had to be set up for two reasons. As a trap and of course for adopting children."

"A trap?" I ask.

"Yes, well we already had a lot of children that needed homes. But with the storm there's been an increase parents dying that kind of thing. But there's also been quite a lot of them being kidnapped, this is the trap we separate them out talk to each one individually and eventually the truth comes out. We've made good progress a lot of children have been reunited with loved ones and a lot of evil people have been arrested."

"Well I told Grace I was going to look after her ever since I found her in those woods."

The administrator smiles. "Well, your employers confirmed you are an employee of theirs and you earn good money which is another box ticked. Where do you live I forgot to ask?"

I tell her but also inform her that I may not be registered there.

"Hmm, okay well I am happy to let you sign the paperwork and take charge as guardian but at some point, you just need to pop in with proof where you live and with Graces birth certificate."

She makes me sign paperwork, then explains that I must cloth her, provide food and look after her wellbeing etc. which I have already been doing anyway.

The administrator also explain I need to transfer Graces parent's estate or assets, but I need a solicitor to do that. She hands me my paperwork and then asks for mobile number for next of kin forms.

I can't find my phone, then Grace hands it to me, she's always somehow got my phone.

The administrator also pulls out a school form for Grace.

I am meant to be listening, but I am confident that Grace can fill me in, so I excuse myself and go to find the officer.

He's not far as he's been eavesdropping. He salutes.

"Ma'am." He says puffing out his chest.

"Can you tell me, did your men see anyone following us?"

"Now that you mention it yes, one of the soldiers seen a car stopped just up the road as you did."

"Well then, when we are ready to leave can you send your men to question them and if I give you the keys to the vehicle out front do you have one out back we can use to get away quietly?"

"Certainly ma'am." We exchange keys and he shows me in the hall where the back door is.

"All done?" I ask the administrator as the conversation has seemed to cease.

Cat looks at the paperwork. "Yep, looks like it, there'll be a team within the next month or so when we get our offices back up and running. They will try to trace any relatives of hers. If they find any relatives they'll be asked if they want to take custody of Grace if they do they'll be court hearing etc. to decide where Grace is best and where Grace would like to be, will be taken into consideration. If no relatives are found, then there still may be a few home visits. Good luck." She says and shakes my hand.

We head out the back, I nod to the officer who starts speaking on his radio.

"Grace, catch." I throw her the keys. "Find the car, it's one of these." I point to a group of four military vehicles. "Honk the horn when you've found it."

I head to the corner of the building, I can't see Grace as there's a van in the way.

Looking around the corner I notice someone's coming a man wearing civilian clothing, but he has his hand suspiciously in his jacket and he looks alert. I guess he's coming for me.

Through a cars reflection I can see that he pulls out a gun as he's about to turn the corner.

I manage to punch his forearm in time, causing him to drop his gun.

He's sees me and goes to punch my face, I manage to block him in time.

I duck his next punch and upper cut him, he spits a tooth on the floor and my knuckles hurt after that one.

His next punch catches me in the ribs, I kick his leg causing him to go to one knee, I can finally get my breath back for a short moment.

He looks left, at his gun. Before I can react, he rolls towards it.

I'm inches away from him before he pulls the trigger. I feel the bullet touch my skin, causing me to stumble into him, the gun ends up back on the floor before he can get a second shot off.

The horn goes off, Grace is in the car. I need to finish this. I manage to get behind him and begin to strangle him.

He gets punches on me, but I keep hold. Finally, he lays limp, unconscious on the floor.

23 PINKIE

I look at my reflection in a wing mirror, my face is unharmed at least Grace won't think anything happened.

Turning the corner, I spot Grace sitting in a military vehicle. My ribs hurt when I walk so does my left thigh.

Once inside the car I quickly speed off down the side street, the soldiers have approached the car and they are shouting.

"What happened to your hand?" Grace asks looking worried.

"I hurt it on a wall."

"You're bleeding." Grace shouts at me in an even more worried voice. She starts crying.

I then feel the warm blood on my ribs, I quickly feel for the wound and find no hole at least.

"It's find it's just a graze." I say but she's still crying. "Grace, I'm fine it's okay." I go to put a hand on her, but she pulls away.

"It's not fine, you lied to me and you could have died." Grace says between sobs. "Well say something." She adds after I can't find something to say.

"Ugh." Grace shouts and looks out the window, crying quietly.

I don't even know what I did wrong, I'm just trying to protect her and myself.

I pull into the shopping centre car park, I'm still applying pressure to my side as it's still bleeding.

"Look Grace." She doesn't look at me. "Please look at me." She does. "I don't want to lie to you but I'm just trying to keep you safe and you shouldn't worry about me I'm good at what I have to do."

"But if you're trying to keep me safe, shouldn't I know what the dangers are? So that if something did happen, I'd be able to deal with it appropriately meaning I could warn you or something."

Honestly sometimes I think she should be the adult.

"Well if I tell you then it's only in case you see something out of place then you run or hide and tell me okay?"

"Okay pinkie swear you'll tell me everything?" Grace asks, wiping away tears.

"Pinkie swear you agree to my terms then?" I ask holding out my pinkie.

Grace scrunches up her face. "Pinkie swear you'll wear a bullet proof vest when you think it's not safe, you can't keep me safe if you're dead and I couldn't cope if I lost you as well." She says looking away from me.

"Deal."

Grace looks back her eyes teary, we link pinkies and shake which causes a smile on her face.

"You okay? You look pale?" Grace asks.

I pull my hand off the wound there's more blood than I thought.

"Help me get to the soldiers over there." I point to a group of soldiers near the shops entrance.

Grace quickly runs around the car and helps me out.

The soldiers salute and quickly help me to a seat in their vehicle.

A soldier approaches me with a med kit and starts seeing to the wound.

"You heard of my presence in the area?" I ask them.

"Yes, ma'am we were told you was in the adoption centre."

The medic finished up.

"Do you have a spare bullet proof vest?" I ask them.

They get one out the boot, Grace smiles at me as I'm keeping my promise.

But I'm going to put it on in a bathroom so I'm not a walking target.

"Is the supermarket open?" I ask as it looks empty, there's also no cars in the car park.

"No, but it is open for an extra hour for military personnel, go on in you should have it to yourselves."

I get my cash out the car and head in. The door beeps as we enter.

Far to the right there's a man on the till, reading a book he doesn't even look up to check who it is.

Grace grabs a trolley.

"Go look at the clothes, I'll be back in a second." She heads to the small clothes section on the left.

I head to the bathroom and lock the door behind me, I lift my top up. My skin is already bruised, and that white bandage is far too big.

Once I put on the bullet proof vest under my top the weight always takes some getting used to and the pain also as it's pressing on my wound and bruises.

I clean up my knuckles and head back to Grace.

Grace is combing through the clothes, taking her time. There's leggings in the trolley but that's all.

"How come you haven't got much?" Grace points to a sign: 'two outfits per person.' "Well pick four and I'll say two are mine if anyone asks."

Grace smiles at that but asks, "Don't you want to buy anything?"

"You've seen how big my clothes bag is." She also smiles at that.

"Okay but you'll let me pick a shoe for you? Your shoe bag was quite small."

"Sure."

Grace finishes up, she's got a dress, skirt and two pairs of jeans her last item is a blue t-shirt with bite me and a cartoon character on.

She picks a military style boot with a short heel for me and picks a shoe for herself. Once done we head for food.

We stand before the many aisles of food, we can't believe how much there is compared to the months of rationing or over priced items.

We go aisle by aisle, getting a lot of food mainly our favourite things that we've been missing.

But as I'm in charge of her health I get healthy meals amongst the junk food, but I don't know how to cook it as I wasn't eating that healthy when I was on my own.

I also manage to hide peanut butter to surprise her later. We also buy a film about a dog.

The cashier looks at me strangely as he puts the clothes through clearly suspicious that two outfits aren't mine as they are somewhat childish.

The soldiers insist and help me load the shopping into the car I give them money and order them to take it.

Okay the healthy food can wait, we change into our comfy pyjamas eat junk food then order a pizza. Once it arrives we eat it while watching the film about a dog which causes us both to cry.

I make my bed as it's big enough for the both of us, as I'm too full from eating too much and I'm too tired to make up Graces bed.

24 GRACE

I wake before her and put the blanket back over her, I bring breakfast back up with me and read while I eat.

Grace wakes in time to eat before it goes cold.

We get ready for the day, we have to go to her home to get her birth certificate, it's an hour's drive away.

The grey city turns to lush green of the countryside. We head through a village. Grace starts to have a worrying look as we get closer.

It seems nice around here, I'd love to live in a place like this but I'm not going to force her to live here just because I'd like to.

"Next left." Grace says and continues to stare out the window.

The left takes me onto a driveway of a large house that sits alone.

By the look of it the house is expensive, there's no car in the driveway so I guess they used it when the storm came.

"Are you coming in? Pick up stuff you want?" I ask.

"I don't want anything from in there if that's okay?" She asks looking at me to say don't make me.

"Yes, that's fine but don't you want your laptop or something?"

Grace looks away, "Everything in there has memories, I want to remember those memories as they were and make new ones with you."

Warms my heart to hear her say she wants to make memories with me, but I'm worried she might regret not taking one last look.

"Okay what do you want me to do with it all? And do you know where a key is to get in?"

"Do whatever you want, sell it if you want and there should be one under the mat."

"Here's the car keys and there's a bottle of water in my bag, I shouldn't be long."

I make my way to the house and find the key under the mat. As I enter the staircase is in front of me, two large rooms to the left and right one room leads to the kitchen.

Where would I keep important documents? In a safe? A safe in the bedroom?

The master bedroom. I head upstairs, I head to the hallway to the left there's three doors and one behind.

One behind me is the bathroom, left room guest room clearly unused, the right room must be Graces room I'll look in there later for anything she might want.

Furthest door leads me to the master bedroom, there's pictures of the three of them all over the walls in different sized picture frames.

Searching the bedroom, I find a box under the bed it reads: 'Grace'.

Upon taking the lid off it's filled with things, I take out a piece of card 'Graces handprints.'

The hand prints are so tiny must have been when she was a baby, there's also footprints.

'First hair ribbon.' This one seems to be from a class project a red ribbon is stuck with tape to a piece of card.

There's more class projects, I find the birth certificate at the bottom, but I'll be taking the box it wouldn't seem right to bin it.

I put a few pictures in the box and head to Graces room, it feels odd rooting around her room when she's just outside.

To make it safely across her room I must tip toe over many items of clothing that's been thrown all over the floor, I sit on her bed which isn't made.

There's a single picture of Grace with her parents all laughing. I place it in the box she should keep.

I find only a laptop of interest in her draws, I once watched a video on how to take out the hard drive which comes in handy now as I should take the hard drive.

There's not much else except pictures, I get to the kitchen and freeze.

There's a man standing in the forest at the end of the garden, he's motioning for me to come.

I take my gun out and decide to see what he wants.

He's garbed in black only his eyes can be seen. He shows me his hand which has the same templar ring, I show him mine.

He hands me a letter still not speaking. He motions to my chest, no my stomach? Both?

"My jacket?" He shakes his head, he motions to say my jacket is a bit to big which is caused by the armour. "Bullet proof vest?"

He nods that I've got it right, then he turns and mounts his horse, then fades into the forest the horse hooves fading away.

I pocket the letter, retrieve the box and lockup the house.

Once in the car I hand Grace the box, she hands me a half empty bottle of water, which I drink as I'm thirsty.

"I didn't know my mother had this." Grace says as she opens the box.

"Well I thought it should be kept."

"It'd be strange if I kept a box about myself."

"Well I'll keep it under my bed and add to it." Grace doesn't object.

We head back to the adoption centre and show the needed documentation and then get the official stamp and ye it's official I've adopted Grace and I'm happy.

Grace is happy but the trip to her home has left a sadness.

I find her sitting on the couch reading still seeming a little down, I retrieve the peanut butter which I forgot to give her.

When I hand it to her the sadness does seem to go away she sits there happily eating it.

Two weeks pass before things seem to get normal more shops open and the trains are back on.

Grace she's settling in, she seems happier, but she won't sleep in her own bed. I don't know if something is wrong.

I receive a letter for an interview in London for the B.P.B. company that I must work for.

Inside the letter there's two train tickets and a reservation letter for a hotel. The dates for a weeks' time.

I inform Grace who seems to be excited.

25 LONDON

The day comes we pack a small bag each, well, we go to, but Grace says her small amount of clothes that she is taking will fit in my bag.

They do fit in my bag but it's heavy I don't complain though maybe I am a pushover only when it comes to Grace.

We take a train into Liverpool then walk to another station, this one has a grand ceiling.

We get onto the London bound train, stow away the bag and get comfy in our seats.

"Can I use your phone?" Grace asks.

"What for?"

"We can listen to music?"

"You can, here." I hand her my phone. "I'm going to get some sleep, wake me if you need me."

Grace take my phone and happily starts searching through it.

Grace tugs at my arm which causes me to wake. A man looks at me, "Tickets?" He asks even though the train stopped meaning aren't we at a station?

I show them to him anyway, he punctures both tickets and leaves.

Ugh, Grace has handed me my phone back and it's dead, I have to ask people the way to the hotel, luckily, it's close by so I don't have to ask many.

"Welcome, do you have a reservation or are you looking for a room?" A woman behind an impressive marble counter.

"I think it's Helena." I hand her the letter after rooting around in my bag.

They type in the details; the phone goes as soon as they finish typing which is a bit suspicious. The woman looks at me then puts the phone down.

"Here is your key card to get into the room, follow me."

There's a short silence in the lift before she finally starts a conversation. "All food is free for BPB agents in the restaurant downstairs. Special guests as well, mainly because of your other employment, room service is also free. We would have also given you the royal suite, but it only has one bed, it's an impressive suite."

"Can we still take it?" Grace asks cheekily.

"If you want, I can go check if it is still available?" The woman asks looking at me for confirmation.

Ugh, I was looking forward to sleeping in a bed on my own, Grace is looking at me with those big adorable eyes. She probably would have somehow squeezed into my bed anyway.

"Sure." I say, it would be good to see if the room is impressive.

"Okay well that's your original room." She motions to a door behind us. "You can wait in there."

I use the card with a beep the door unlocks, Grace sits on the closest bed and begins to bounce on it as if she is testing how comfy it is.

"I hope the bed is as comfy as this." Grace says continuing to bounce on it.

The woman returns a few minutes later, "If you'd follow me, I'll take you to your new room."

We head to the top floor, the woman motions for me to do something but I don't know what it is.

Grace takes the card off me and swipes a pad above the elevator buttons.

The elevator doors open to a large room, a four-poster bed with gold legs sits in the centre of the room.

Either side of the bed double doors lead to a balcony.

There's a couch to the right and a TV on the wall. The couch also looks expensive everything in the room oozes wealth.

"Do you require anything else?" The woman asks.

"No thanks."

When she leaves I drop onto the bed face first, it's surprisingly comfy.

There's not much of the day left, so we get into our pyjamas, we should put the duvet and any pillows we can find onto the couch, so that it's comfy guess they bought it to look good not for how comfy it is.

With much persuasion from Grace I eventually allow her to paint my nails a matt black, while we watch a film which they may charge me for but worth it.

That night I get the best sleep in a long time except Grace now and then nudging me or stealing the duvet.

As my phone has been on charge overnight Grace uses it to take pictures of the impressive view and we also take a selfie.

I catch my matt black nails in the light, I like them is Grace making me soft if so I like the change.

Is my heart growing like a certain green person in a movie, if it is then I'm glad.

My interview is not until late afternoon, so we have most of the day to ourselves we've planned to go sightseeing.

Over lunch Grace reminds me I still need a solicitor which reminds me that I need to call Roxy which makes me anxious.

Finally, the time comes, we're standing outside the BPB headquarters.

"Ow." Grace shouts, I squeezed her hand to hard by accident I think she knows that as she doesn't let go. I use my thumb and reassuringly trace a circle on her palm.

We head in to the grand marble lobby. Four guards stand at the sides with guns a single desk at the end sits a man in front of a computer.

"Welcome to the British Protection Bureau, how may I help?" The man asks as we approach, looking over his glasses at us.

"I have an interview." I say.

"Name?"

"Helena."

He types into his computer. "That elevator thirty first floor." He says pointing at an elevator.

We stand in the lift the door opens on the thirty first floor. This floor is busy with people running about, another receptionist also waits I give my name.

This time we are told to sit in the waiting area.

A woman approaches, she looks the same age as me, her jet-black hair gives off a shine as the light touches it, I'm jealous of her hair.

"Hello Helena, it's very good to meet you." I remember her voice, I shake her hand. "And this must be Grace, right?" Grace nods and she shakes her hand. "My name is Megan, Helena if you'd like to follow me, Grace can stay here. Gena can look after her." She motions to the assistant. "Gena can you get Grace a hot chocolate and she can eat my biscuits from the kitchen."

Megan leads me past various sized offices to her office which is much larger than the rest.

"Sit, sit." Megan says, I'm sitting on a sofa a comfy one, she takes a seat behind a desk.

"So," Megan begins. "This is more of an induction rather than an interview as I've been told you have to work with us for." She types on her laptop. "Ah, for a minimum of one year then the choice is yours, oh wait I was also told to give you this." Megan slides an envelope over to me.

"What is it?" I ask but Megan raises her hands in a I don't know sort of way.

There's a wax seal stamped with the templar logo.

A square card falls out one word: 'Apologies.' And a letter which reads: 'Sorry for Jeff's theatrics in the forest, hope your new armour fits you well.'

The letter from that man in the forest, the letter in my bag which I left with Grace.

"Something the matter?" Megan asks, I want to retrieve my bag, do I trust her, I must if I must talk to her for a year. Besides she saved me from that Lieutenant when she didn't need to.

I tell her about what's happened since she enlisted me to that splinter army to get me out of prison and about the man in the forest.

"Sit." Megan says as I stand up to go get my bag, she picks up the phone. "Gena can you send Grace to my office."

A few minutes later Grace enters holding a hot chocolate with my bag on her shoulder, she smiles at me and takes a seat on a separate couch on the back wall.

I search my bag and find the envelope.

It's got an address written on it, I don't recognize the area code.

"Do you know where this is?" I ask Megan handing her the letter.

"Yes, it's in the London a book shop I think." She types in the address on her laptop and turns the screen towards me.

It's a bookstore hmm. "I'll call you a taxi to take you there once we are finished here if you want?"

"Sure, that would be great, thanks."

"Okay well back to business, you don't hold a driving license am I correct?" I nod. "Well as it's what you'll be doing most every day I'll call our advanced driving school in Liverpool; two weeks and you'll have a license."

"Two weeks, I'll need time to find a car." I say.

"No, I pick that for you it has to be expensive, fast and armoured slightly or fully. You'll find it parked outside your house in the next few days, you'll have to sign for it and then it's yours."

"Mine?" I like the sound of expensive.

"Yes, we get car donations from wealthy people, even if you leave us after a year the car is still yours."

A free armoured, fast, expensive car I can't complain.

"You will also have to do a five-day combat training, which also includes first aid. Which will take you up to a total of three weeks then you'll have a week off. Then by a months' time your duties will start."

"What are my duties?"

"Well protection of course you guessed that, you'll be driving around client's children as they are at risk of being kidnapped for ransom. I've got a month to work out your schedule, but each day you will be ferrying three children, dropping them off at school and picking them up when they finish. During the day you'll sit in a designated safe house watching CCTV unless one of our clients need to be escorted to an airport that sort of thing. On rare occasions you will be asked to work a night shift but if you do the next day you'll have off. That's it basically, I do have to give you this sixty-page booklet though."

"What's in it?"

"A lot of legal stuff."

"So, I work for you?"

Megan sits back in her chair.

"Both of us work for BPB obviously but we work with each other, an assistant has one agent that's you the agent. I tell you where to be etc. But I can also tend to personal matters for you, say you need a plumber I can arrange appointments like that if you are too busy to."

"What happened to your previous agent?"

"He left to work overseas, for better pay." There's a short silence. "Is there anything of a personal matter I can sort out for you?"

"Well, can you extend our stay at the hotel, for another night?"

Megan stops slouching and sits upright and starts typing in her laptop. "Done. It's none of my business but is it because you like the room or? And between us usually personal reasons cost you, this time I'll charge the company."

"No, I need work clothes and the shops by us aren't open and if it's between us Grace also needs more clothes."

"All the shops are back open here, as it is London."

Megan makes me sign several documents, then tells me she'll post the sixty-page document as I can't be carrying it around with me.

We chat while waiting for a taxi, I find out she has a dad that she never sees as he lives overseas.

"Oh wait." Megan says as we begin to leave. "Your BPB badge if anyone stops you when carrying a weapon. And a gift from myself not the company, family friendly of course, it's for tonight so you'll have time to go to the book store."

It's two cinema tickets, but did she just give me a badge to allow me to carry my weapons? Finally, I don't have to hand over a card with a number on.

"Thanks." I say and hug, what made me hug her, I blame it on Grace she's turned me into a hugger.

26 BOOKSTORE

We head in the taxi to the bookstore.

It's out of the way, in a rich residential part.

Two shop windows show multiple books, we head in.

"Looking for a book?" A man behind the counter asks.

"No, I have a letter."

"Oh?" I hand it over. "Your hand." What? My hand. "Your hand." He says again.

I place both on the counter, he picks up my hand with the ring on. He places it gently back on the table then hurries to the door and flips the open sign around and locks the door.

"Follow me."

We turn this way and that, getting lost in the continuous bookshelves.

Eventually we stop at a dead end.

"Stand there."

I stand on a spot that looks like a stain on the floor, a camera appears on the bookshelf and begins to scan me.

A 3D scan of myself appears on a screen my name underneath it.

The bookshelf swings inwards, there's a stand with armour on it.

It's thinner than normal body armour it doesn't seem to have the usual Kevlar plates.

"It's much thinner than a normal vest." He begins. "There's no strike plate as the whole thing is a strike plate, it is heavier though. It's designed for its low profile, so you can wear it under a suit or a dress and it won't give you that bulky look, it will just look normal, like you're just wearing a suit or a dress. It has memory material, so it moulds to your body shape. Because of the thinner strike plates if you do get shot it'll leave a nastier bruise than normal, possibility of broken bones. It won't stop a fifty-calibre bullet though."

"What are these?" I ask, some sort of stretchy material.

"They go on your thighs, they don't stop bullets, but it will slow them down and if a bullet does enter through the material it tightens to stop the blood. Deaths have been decreased when soldiers have been wearing these. We had a neck one as well, but it didn't work, sometimes the material would choke people."

"What's that?" I ask as a red flashing light begins to pulsate.

"They're coming." He looks like he's just witnessed his own death.

"Who?"

"I can't say it's not my place, can you help me defend?"

"Yes, as long as there's somewhere for Grace to go?"

"In there with the armour, that room is bomb proof, bullet proof and it has its own air supply."

"Yes, yes that's fine." I bend down as Grace climbs in, so I can look at her in the eyes. "Look, don't come out of there no matter what you hear, wait until I get you out okay?" She looks at me scared.

"Pinkie swear that you'll come back then." Clearly, she means don't die.

I lock pinkies with her and shake, she goes into the room and squashes up next to the armour. I slowly carefully close the door on her.

"You got a spare vest? I don't want to wear my new one yet." I ask him when I find him back at the counter looking at CCTV images, he throws one to me.

"Choose your weapon." He says as a painting behind the counter lifts, revealing a stash of weapons.

I grab a semi-automatic and a shotgun which I secure with a strap over my shoulder. I stuff a pistol under my belt at the back, just in case.

"How many?" I ask now that he's finally turned off the warning light which was starting to make me nervous.

"Three cars, fifteen max, minimum three." I hope it's the minimum.

I hear the cars racing down the road, then the screeching of their tires as the cars come to a sudden stop.

Then the shattering of the glass as they immediately open fire.

The gun fire stops, which allows us to pop our heads up and return fire.

It goes on like that for a short while until they have time to advance.

We down the first few that come through the door and windows before the rest take cover inside the store.

I hear the click of my gun, out of ammo and there's no more.

The shop owner is telling me to flank, we are at a disadvantage being so close to each other.

I move, keeping low and hide behind a bookshelf, I retrieve the shotgun and begin to fire.

My last shotgun shell catches a man in the chest dead or not I can't tell, but is he getting up anytime soon, probably not.

His friends rush me and punch me before I can get the gun out the back of my belt.

I'm still holding the shotgun which I use as a club, it catches one in the head, he immediately drops to the floor.

The last charges into me sending us both to the floor and the shotgun is out of reach.

My right hands trapped behind my back, it hurts but that's where my gun is.

The man headbutts me, I punch at him with my left hand, he gets some serious punches to my body before I'm able to pull my trapped hand free, holding the gun.

I quickly squeeze the trigger; his body lies motionless on top of me. I roll him off and stand up.

Everybody is either dead or passed out, but I can't see the store man.

I find him hunched behind the counter, clutching his stomach, he coughs several times.

"You must go," he stops to cough. "You can't be here when the police arrive."

"But…"

"Go, I'll be fine."

His minds made up, so I get to Grace and the armour.

I make sure Grace closes her eyes so that she doesn't see the many bodies.

We reach the street and a car screeches to a halt before us, I immediately reach for a gun, but I don't have one.

"Megan sent me, get in." I hesitate, what if it's a trap, then I hear the sirens and get in the back with Grace.

The driver takes us a few streets away and pulls over.

"Here." He says and throws a phone to me.

"Are you two okay?" It's Megan.

"Yeah, I'm bruised and dirty, but besides that we're okay."

"I heard a police scanner, they were responding to a disturbance at a bookstore, another assistant, a friend owed me a favour. The driver, he's new, his first job. He'll take you wherever you want."

"Okay, thanks for the help, take care." I hang up and pass him his phone back.

"Where to then?" He asks.

"Ho-"

"No," Grace cuts me off. "Can we still go to the cinema?"

"But look at the state of me."

"I know, but we were having a good time until this happened, can we please pretend it didn't happen, please?"

"Okay, take me to the cinema then." I say, Grace puts her head in my lap, I gently place my hand on top.

At the cinema I freshen up in the bathroom, I can't do much with my hair, so I just brush it.

There's also a few cuts one visible on my cheek and a bruise under my eye, the staff look at me like I've just came from an action movie.

We watch the film, it's about superheroes, I must admit it does take my mind off what just happened.

The car is still waiting when we get out it takes us straight to the hotel.

"Will you be needing me in the morning?" The driver asks.

"Yep, only in the morning at ten please."

We head back into the lobby.

"Helena, welcome. You'll be staying an extra night?"

It's the same woman from the other day.

"Yes, we head home the day after tomorrow is that correct?" I ask to make sure.

She quickly types into the computer. "Yes, you are correct."

"Thanks."

We retire to our room. I can't wait to get a shower, ease my aching bones.

"You still want to go shopping, tomorrow don't you?" I ask Grace, even though I probably already know the answer.

Grace nods and I was right, after her speech I guessed she would.

We watch movies, but I watch from the bed as I'm sure I'm going to fall asleep at any time which I do.

27 PHONE CALL

I wake and find that the duvets been put over me.

Grace is sitting in her pyjamas at the small circle table in the corner.

"I ordered room service." Grace says as she notices me sitting up. "There's enough for you as well."

I put on my dressing gown and join her, the first thing I notice is the mountain of pancakes in the centre and syrup on top.

We eat until we can't possibility eat another, it's nearly ten se we change.

The BPB agent takes us to the city centre and drops us off, he informs us that he'll be at the hotel room tomorrow at nine to take us back to Liverpool.

We head to various clothes stores, buying Grace clothes, eventually Grace stops and scrunches up her face with an odd expression.

"This is strange you haven't bought anything."

"I don't need anything from these stores, the last shop I'm going to buy work clothes."

"Well at least let me buy you something."

"Okay but I've got to agree on it."

"Can I have your card? It would be odd if you did buy it yourself." She says with an outstretched hand looking at me with an odd expression.

Am I really going to do this, give a child my bank card and pin number, fine I trust her anyway and we are going to be living together, so I hand it over.

"Don't lose it." I add.

Grace makes me try on several dresses, finally settling on a black one that ends above the knee, also a light grey skirt with a white long-sleeved top.

I agree to all as it looks good on me.

Finally, we get back to buying her things, she taps on my shoulder to get my attention.

"Can I get my ears pierced?"

"Of course, if you want. Go find a staff member."

Grace comes back with a staff member who tells her to jump on the seat, which she does. She holds my hand as the person pierces her ears, she squeezes my hand in anticipation then seems to let go when she realizes it didn't hurt that much.

When asked if she wants to buy earring studs I allow her to, she chooses a circle kind, I can see her eyeing up a pair of diamond ones I know she won't ask as they are expensive.

"Go and finish searching the store for clothes." I say pulling a face at her, which she laughs at, I buy the diamond earing studs, I know, I know I'm spoiling her, but I can't help it.

The last shop I buy my work clothes, black pants that sort of thing.

We stand outside the shop and I have over the bag with the diamond studs in and hand it to Grace.

"What's this?" Grace asks, looking surprised.

"Open it."

She gets excited and hugs me when she opens it. "Thanks." She says and hugs me again. This child has an expensive taste it's dangerous.

We decide to go to a gadget shop last, we both want to check out the latest gadgets. I buy a laptop as she'll need it for school. I also buy her a new phone with much persuasion as she said she didn't need one which I knew was a lie.

When I hand Grace her phone, she looks pleased it has a large screen which she says will be good for watching things on.

I also get a tablet and a gigantic impressive TV, but I get that delivered to the house, it cost a lot as it's a 4K TV. I thought why not get it. Grace and I enjoy watching films together. Also, we play on a few games consoles, I'm considering buying her one as she seems to enjoy it but enough gifts for one day.

We go to a certain fast food restaurant which has nice burgers, Grace does seem to be enjoying herself which makes me feel good as my job as her guardian I think should be ensuring she's happy.

We decide to take a taxi back as we have too many shopping bags.

A receptionist at the hotel insists and helps carry the bags to our room.

We watch another film in our PJ's but go to sleep early as we need to wake early tomorrow.

Making sure we haven't left anything, we leave and wait in the lobby, eventually the agent walks in and where on our way home.

I call Megan as soon as we are home, I notice the military vehicle is gone, I need an extension before I do my driving test.

"What for?" Megan asks.

"I need to sort Graces affairs, her parents' house mainly."

"You need a solicitor then?"

"Yes."

"I can get you the best."

"No, I have someone in mind."

"Okay, well next week Monday you'll start but I can't delay any longer."

"That's fine, I won't need more than the week, thank you."

Now I must call Roxy. She might not want to speak to me, I was meant to call her a few months back, but I was stupid and only wanted my own company.

I find her number and my palms are getting sweaty as I wait for her to pick up.

Maybe she doesn't have her phone due to the storm as she doesn't pick up and it goes to voicemail, I decide to try again.

"Hello." Its Roxy.

"Hello, Its Helena."

I hear her sigh.

"I'm sorry I didn't call," I say. "I was stupid not to call and things got busy."

"Oh." Roxy says like she doesn't want to talk, or rather doesn't want to talk to me.

"I shouldn't have called, I'm sorry."

"No, no, I'm sorry. I should hear you out at least. In person though, my house. You know where it is?"

"Again, I'm sorry but no." I feel bad I don't know where she lives.

Roxy gives me her address.

"I have a plus one hope you don't mind."

"You found yourself a boyfriend then?"

"No, it's my daughter Grace. Well I adopted her, so not daughter but close enough." Daughter I feel stupid, it just slipped out. But I would be proud if she was, I am proud of her.

"Interesting, not to sound rude but I never had you for the caring type."

"Me either."

"Okay well you'll have to tell me all about it. A proper catch up but don't brush me off this time." There's a sense of anger in the last part which is fair enough.

"I won't, I promise."

"Well come the day after tomorrow."

"Okay."

We say our goodbyes and end the call.

How am I going to get there without a car, it's an hour walk and like a ten to fifteen-minute drive.

I'll walk if I must, but I'll call Megan tomorrow see where the car is.

28 CAR

"Stay here." I tell Grace as she wakes up as there's a knock on the door.
I grab my dressing gown and head for the door.

"Delivery for Helena."

"Oh yes, the TV?"

"Yeah, sign here." He hands me a clip board.

He comes back, him and his colleague are holding the TV, carefully taking their steps.

"We can install it on a wall for fifty pounds if you'd like?"

I look at the wall where I want it, Grace couldn't help me put it up its far too heavy for her, or if she could it could get broken.

"Yes please." I pay them and tell them where I want it, I make them tea and thank them when they finish.

Grace comes down and starts flicking through the channels.

I go to call Megan.

"Yes, the car should be there today." She says.

"Am I able to drive it?"

There's a short silence.

"I'm not... Call me on my personal phone."

Megan gave me a different number and I call.

"The company records all calls on business line. Anyway, I'm not supposed to tell you this until you get your license, but you have diplomatic plates."

"So, I can drive it?"

"I'm already breaking rules for you and we've only been working together for a week. You're not a good influence, so yes you can just don't turn up to the driving school they'll have you arrested."

"Okay I won't."

"And Helena don't crash it please, it probably costs the same as a small house and you're not even meant to be driving. Plus, if you were injured I'd be unhappy with myself and I would have to do tons of paperwork."

"I won't crash it, I promise."

"Okay, take care."

"You too."

I'm dressed and waiting excited for what car it is.

There's a knock on the door, before I was about to make dinner.

A man in a suit, is waiting.

"Helena?" He asks and then seems to compare me to an image he has on his tablet he's holding.

"Fingerprint there and signature there." He says pointing. "If you'd come with me, I also need a picture of you next to the car."

I'm having to compose myself the car looks so nice it's a big off road looking, it even has a step to get into the car.

He hands me the keys says goodbye and leaves.

I climb into the car; the leather seats are quite comfy. The car has that new smell.

There's a manual on the dashboard, I flick through it. I'll take a proper look later.

Although I stop on a page heated seats, I'm in love with the car, I turn the heated seats on.

I go to get Grace while the seats are warming.

"Now? I'm in my pyjamas and jogging pants." She says like I've just said something criminal.

"So, just put a jacket on we're just going for a drive."

Grace agrees and quickly helps me lock up the house.

"Woah." She says upon seeing the car. "You know how much that car is? Just the standard version?"

"Nope."

"Like, ninety thousand."

"What! That's crazy."

"Yep," she says still looking at the car. "And yours is definitely not the standard version."

"Climb in then, we'll go for a drive."

Ah, the seat is so comfy, it's nice and warm.

The car glides smoothly over bumps and potholes.

"Would you like to go to a restaurant for dinner?" I ask after we've been driving for a while.

"But I'm in my PJ's." She looks at me, again like I've just asked her to do something criminal.

"Yeah, I can find a quiet pub, or you can borrow my jumper again."

"But you'll be cold you're only wearing a jumper and a jacket?"

"I'll just wear my jacket. I'll be fine." Grace worries too much or is this what it's like to care for each other.

"Deal, if you're sure." Will she ever stop borrowing my clothes, to be fair this was my fault.

We find a quiet pub, the owner compliments me on my car although they look oddly at me when I don't take my jacket off when we begin to eat.

Grace talks about school luckily, I have the week off the day after tomorrow we must go to this Courtsfield High and see if she can get into it.

On the way back, we get a tail, which gives me a chance to test the speed of the vehicle.

It's fast, we easily lose the tail and are back at home in time to watch a film on the new TV with hot chocolate, snuggled up on the couch with blankets. But I still want to know who the tail was, I can't take my mind of it.

29 OLD FRIEND

I wake on the couch with Grace on me.

Roxy didn't give a time so I'm in no rush.

Once we are ready we head to the shop to buy a bottle of wine as a gift for Roxy. Then we head to Roxy's house.

It's in a cul-de-sac, quite a large house, I park in her driveway and knock on the door.

I'm nervous again, I hope she does truly forgive me for not calling.

"Hello." Roxy says as an automatic response when she opens the door. "Come in, come in."

We step inside and close the door behind us.

"I got this as a gift." I hand her the bottle of wine.

Roxy smiles at it.

"My favourite, you remembered. Remember when we were teenagers and we drank two bottles of this and we were constantly puking." She looks at the bottle. "I'm no alcoholic but I could probably handle more."

"Yes, I remember, I'd hold your hair back and as soon as you'd finish you would do the same for me."

We both smile at that, they were good times minus the puking.

"Sorry where are my manners, you must be?" Roxy asks holding out her hand towards Grace.

"Grace." She says and shakes her hand.

"That's a very nice bracelet."

"It's Helena's actually."

"Oh." She looks at me and I look back like I'll explain later.

"Well I also have someone for you to meet. Lexie come down here please." Roxy shouts the last part.

A girl appears at the top of the stairs, she pushes her brunette hair out of her face then realizes there's guests and ties her dressing gown tighter.

"What?" Lexie says in a moody manner, she looks the same age as Grace.

"This is my friend Helena and her adopted daughter Grace, and this is my adopted daughter Lexie."

"Hello." Lexie says.

"Lexie why don't you show Grace your room?"

"Okay. Come on." Lexie says and disappears.

Grace looks at me then heads up the stairs after her.

Roxy leads me into the living room where we sit on the couch.

"Would you like a glass of wine?"

"No, I'm the designated driver."

"You drive?" She asks.

"Yes, what do you think is in your driveway?"

"What." Roxy puts down the bottle of wine and heads to the window parting the blinds.

"How did you afford that?" She asks scrunching up her face. "Sorry, I shouldn't have asked about your finances."

"No, no it's fine. I got it for free actually."

I tell her everything once I do she sits back in the chair and takes a long swig from her wine glass.

"Well I feel bad now for being mad at you for not calling."

"No, I should, I should have called."

"Nonsense we hadn't spoke for a while and you had a lot on your plate, I insist you have a drink with me."

Roxy shoves a drink in my hand.

"I can't I have to drive home, and I've got to go with Grace to see if she can get into a high school."

"What high school?"

"Courtsfield High."

"The same as Lexie." She says. "You must stay the night then, we can all go together tomorrow afternoon."

"Hmm, okay but I'll need to go back to mine in the morning you and Lexie can come."

"That's fine."

"Looks like we will have a good night then."

While drinking she tells me her and Lexie had an argument that morning over her diabetes injection. That's why she seemed a bit moody. Apparently, she's a bit reckless by taking the injection a little late which is making Roxy worried.

I must have dozed off my boots are off and I'm on the couch with a blanket over me.

I put my boots on and head to the kitchen, Roxy's sitting at the dining table.

"Morning." She says.

"Morning." I say. "What happened last night?"

"You had some more wine and dozed off when we were watching a film. You are still a light weight."

"Always a light weight you know that. Have you seen Grace?"

"Still in Lexie's room, she also dozed off. Both are still asleep, I'll wake them soon. Cereal is over there if you want some."

I grab a cereal bowl, pour the cereal then the milk and sit opposite Roxy.

"Where's your husband?" I ask. "I noticed pictures on your wall and your ring on your finger."

"Oh, he's away on business, I hardly see him. He calls often, Lexie hasn't even met him yet."

"Business?"

"Yes, he's in Scotland now, then London, then I think he goes overseas." She says looking away, I can tell it bothers her.

"I don't want to over step, how come you didn't have a baby you always talked about it?"

"He didn't want one but as I grew older I didn't mind really, then he's always away even when the storm happened, so I adopted. He's not happy, probably why he extended his trip."

"Oh."

"Yep." She says and continues to eat. "I'm going to jump in the shower. You can have the fun job of waking the girls." She smiles.

Why do I get that job, it's like an evil necessary job?

I finish my cereal and head up the stairs, they are both asleep in Lexie's bed. Grace must have borrowed Lexie's PJ'S.

"Wake up you two, come on." I say gently shaking them, generating only some movement. I open the curtains which does cause them to squirm and wake.

"You both want cereal?" I receive a nod and a croaky ye. "Ok, well get up it will be on the table downstairs."

I head back down and put two bowls on the table, Lexie comes down first, she smiles at me and I smile back.

Grace comes down second dressed in her own clothes. They eat in silence as there's not much to say.

Roxy comes back down. "Ready to go then?" She asks. "Lexie, you got your paperwork?"

"You're the adult you should know what paperwork is needed."

I feel like an argument could happen at any moment.

"We'll wait in the car, come on Grace." I say quickly.

The car warms up while we wait, Grace is sitting in front with me.

Roxy and Lexie climb in the back.

We head back to my house, Roxy says the house looks nice, but her house is bigger. She's also impressed with the TV quality.

I take a quick shower change and then find all paperwork with Grace.

Grace and Lexie climb in the back of the car and share headphones, they must be listening to music.

We head to the high school, it looks like, well a high school, so depressing.

I pull into the car park, okay maybe my car does look expensive especially compared to these.

When we step out the car we notice the giant signs, visitors this way.

The signs take us to a large gymnasium, many desks are dotted about the place.

"Take a seat at a desk and someone will be along shortly." A man at the entrance informs us.

There's already several people seated and in deep conversation.

We sit at a table, Roxy sits at a table close by.

"Hello." A man says on approach to us. "I'm Mr. Breakley and you are?"

We give our names, he writes them on name tags and gives them to us. I help Grace attach hers to her top as she's having trouble.

"Are you a teacher here?" I ask.

"Yes, I teach math, ugh who likes math right." He smiles at Grace. "You are looking to study at Courtsfield High then?"

"Yep." Grace says.

"Well you are lucky, we are giving away place, we reserve the last hundred places for late comers who'll have to come through a more thorough process."

"So, she has a place here then?"

"Yep, a few things to fill in first, then a tour and a start date."

I fill in several forms without incident, incident meaning I didn't panic because I had the necessary information.

The only one that gets me is emergency contact I need three.

"Can it be anyone?" I ask him.

"Well, not anyone, it's your daughter's life. But I know what you mean, so yes, we usually prefer it to be relatives but if you have no one, then it can be anyone you trust."

"Can I just go over there then, I want to ask before I go ahead?" Why am I asking, it just happened if he said no I'd either leave or do it anyway.

"You know them? Yes of course that's fine."

I head over to Roxy, I ask her and she's fine with it, she stops me before I go to sit back down.

"Can I put you down as a second?" Roxy asks. "My husband can go third."

"Yeah, sure." I say, I understand that she currently has problems with her husband.

Megan can go third, she seemed to genuinely care about the both of us and she is constantly near her phone. I've never been put on voicemail, but I'll have to tell her later and hope she's okay with it.

"Well, all the paperwork is done you will get a confirmation in the post." He slides a piece of paper across the table. "That's a uniform list and where to buy them." He looks at his watch. "As you know them two, is it okay if I leave you with Mrs. Mc Nare you can have the tour together?"

"Yes, that's fine." I say, he gathers up the paperwork and heads off.

We sit waiting until they are finished. Once they are, Mc Nare looks at us all and picks up the paperwork and says, "If you'd follow me then, I need to drop these off at the office, then we'll go on the tour."

Mrs Mc Nare hands off the paperwork to a receptionist and then begins to show us around.

First, we stop at the IT rooms, which she states is one of the best in the area, they are high spec she also informs us the school is an IT and PE specialist.

Each classroom has tablets to aid learning although the teacher makes sure that Grace and Lexie know they need stationary to write on paper and pencils to draw especially in art.

The next room is the cookery room it smells like fresh bread which is what we are offered, and it tastes nice.

The last room is a woodwork room, Grace seems to like the idea of when they make items out of wood they sell it and the proceeds go to charity.

A shiver runs down my spine as I notice someone looking at me through the window they are looking at me I'm sure, they seem to have a sinister smile on their face.

Luckily, they are gone when it's time to leave.

Mc Nare informs us that they start next month which is a few weeks away, but she said the letter should be clearer.

30 FIRST DAY

We head to the supermarket as Roxy wants to get a few things, but we get another tail ugh.

I won't be able to lose them there's too much traffic these days.

"Go on ahead." I say to Roxy as we climb out the car, I need to call Megan see what I should do. "Grace come here a second." I hand her my bank card. "Get what you want and get me a bag of those crisps I like, you know the ones?"

She nods we hug and she runs after Roxy.

"Megan!" I say when she picks up the phone.

"Hello to you too." Megan says sarcastically.

"Sorry, Hello."

"What's up?" she asks.

"I keep getting a tail, usually I lose them, but I can't today, and I can't keep my house guarded and Roxy's house."

"Right, you need to all stay at your house, we have procedure for this sort of thing, we will send a car to watch your house."

"Thanks again, oh I had to put you name down for an emergency contact for Graces school hope you don't mind?"

"No problem, and no I don't mind."

"Okay good, take care."

Now I must convince Roxy to stay at mine, I go find her in the supermarket.

"I was thinking have you got Lexie's uniform?"

"No not yet, I need to soon. I go back to work next week."

"Then now I insist you stay at mine tonight and we'll go tomorrow?"

Roxy hesitates, "Yeah, okay." She says.

Well that was easier than I thought it was going to be.

We get a movie, snacks and Roxy insists more wine.

I notice the BPB agents waiting outside my house, they wave at me.

Another night I enjoy, even if I ended up again not having my bed to myself. Roxy and I finished the wine while talking on my bed resulting in both of us falling asleep.

We head to the store to pick up their uniforms and no one tails the car which is a good sign, maybe they got the hint to stop following me.

The store we are heading to only deals in uniforms, how they make their money all year round I have no idea. I buy her PE uniform and school uniform, she must wear a blazer she looks like she belongs in a law firm.

The next weeks are quite fun, I do advanced driving they have a car which they shoot at while I'm driving, bullet proof of course.

They even have explosives going off and pursuit vehicles that chase me.

I receive my driving license, it's got a mug shot of me, Grace finds it funny.

Each day I head home and feed the two monsters, Grace and Lexie, I pick Lexie up each day and drop her off at mine. Roxy and I are at work or training during the day so we both thought it best if they were in the same house, which luckily, they both don't mind.

Plus, Megan insists BPB agents sit outside, even though the tails have gone they still don't know who it was. I have no way of asking the Templar order either to see if they know.

The gun and unarmed combat is also fun, but my instructors say I am a natural and I pick it up easily resulting in the sessions being cut short.

The week that I have off at the end of the training, I take Grace and Lexie out, for walks mostly and spoiling them but I can't help it. I also buy Lexie a few books, Grace said she is still busy reading the mass number of books that encase my room.

My alarm goes off, it's seven in the morning. My first day of official duties and it's Graces first day of high school.

I wake Grace up and then get dressed, this time I also wear my holsters. Going to need my guns.

Grace takes a while to get dressed, I've got dressed, brushed my teeth and now I'm eating breakfast and she's still in her room.

Eventually she comes down in her skirt and blazer looking smart.

"Have you seen my shoes?" She asks.

"By the door I think."

Grace puts on her shoes and sits at the table and eats her cereal I prepared for her.

"Oh, come on, stand up." I say.

"Why?" Grace asks with a mouthful of cereal.

"I need to take a picture to add to your mum's box of mementos."

"Okay, but only if we use your mirror in your room to take a picture together, it's you first day as well."

"Deal."

Firstly, I help her do her tie she has never done one before and after several attempts of showing her how it's done she still can't get the hang of it, so I do it for her.

I take a picture of her, I'm going to write first day of high school when I get a chance to print it off.

We then take a picture together, after several re-takes she finds the one she likes and makes me send it to her.

I set my background picture of Grace, it means if anyone asks I can quickly show them and tell them how proud I am of her.

We pick up Lexie on the way, Roxy doesn't have a car and she doesn't start work until late, so we decided I can pick her up and drop her off.

When I pull into the bay to drop them off, I hear Lexie ask, "Helena can you help me please?" Lexie's holding her tie.

"Sure." I say turning in my seat, Lexie sits on the edge of her seat, so I can reach her neck.

Lexie tells me she lied to Roxy and told Roxy she could tie it herself, which puts me in a difficult position do I tell Roxy and break Lexie trust. I decide I won't just in case she needs someone in the future, I don't want her thinking she can't turn to me, plus she does feel guilty as Lexie admits she shouldn't have lied.

"Thanks." Lexie says when I finish up and jumps out the car.

"Have a good day." I say to them both.

Grace grabs her bags and kisses me on the cheek, before following Lexie into the school its then I realize people looking at me or rather looking at the car.

I drive off quickly, now I must go to an address close by to pick up the first client.

Arriving at the gates a person's voice shouts from a speaker, "Who is it?"

"Helena, BPB agent." I take out my badge and hold it up to the camera.

The gates swing inwards to the large house with its many windows and a door with decorative artwork.

A man with black glasses speaks into his sleeve, a boy aged probably eight or nine stands in front of him.

His body guard opens the door, the boy climbs in the back without speaking clearly not his first time.

I take him to a school close by, but the school is no ordinary school, they have guards who open the door after giving me a key word that I was expected to hear.

I watch the boy go up the steps and into the school, I must for procedure.

I have one more pickup, another rich neighbourhood a girl this time, seventeen maybe eighteen.

"I can get the door myself." I hear her say in a posh accent as she opens the door.

"You enjoy your job?" She asks me.

"My first day, enjoying it so far." I spoke to soon we got a tail different from the other day. "Hope you have your seatbelt on."

My car accelerates quickly, I'm grateful for the diplomatic plates as I break the speed limit quickly and lose the tail.

"Are you okay?"

"Yes, a little shaken."

We've arrived at the college.

"Where are the guards?"

"We don't have them outside, we use iris scanners and fingerprint, there's also a safe room in the basement, I'll be safe." She says.

"Fine, but I'm escorting you to the door." I do and watch through the door to make sure there is an eye scanner, which there is.

Next, I head to the safe house where I sit and listen to the police scanner. There's several BPB agents here but they all seem to know each other and look at me like I don't belong here which I admit is odd.

I also must fill out an after-action report from the tail I received.

I pick them up again to drop them at home, first the college girl as she finished early then the boy, then that's me finished for the day.

31 GALA

Now, I go to pick up Lexie and Grace.

I've been waiting a while and yes getting stares, then I see them both approaching.

"Had a good day?" I ask.

"We had tests already." Grace complains.

"Already?"

"Yeah, they need to see what we know as we haven't been in school for a year."

"Helena?" Lexie says questioningly.

"Yeah?"

"Grace told me you have guns."

"Well she shouldn't have." I say softly and move my blazer, so she can see the holsters.

"Cool." Lexie says when she sees them. "Does Roxy know?"

"Yes, she said you couldn't be in safer hands. But the both of you must promise me you won't tell any of your classmates. I'm serious only we can know okay?"

I get an okay from both.

We pull up outside Roxy's and then I get a phone call from Roxy.

"I'm going to be late home can you feed Lexie?"

"Of course."

I pass the phone to Lexie as she wants to ask her about her day and drive home while they talk.

I think Roxy is good at her job and her employer takes advantage of it, they always make her work after hours.

I call Megan to see if I can get tomorrow off as it's an inset day and Grace has been asking me for a while to help paint her room, even threatening to do it herself as we've had the paint ready for a while.

"There is a night time job, it means you'll get tomorrow off." Megan informs me.

"I'll take it, what's the job?"

"A charity Gala, BPB are providing the security, but you will need to pick up one of the donators, he contributes a lot of money to BPB. You will also have to stay close to him inside the venue."

"I can wear a dress then?"

"Yes, it's a formal occasion."

"What time?"

"The event officially finishes at twelve, I'll text you the address and a time."

I've probably got a few hours to get ready. I leave them to eat.

I change into the black dress Grace bought me. I have the new bullet proof vest underneath and looking in the mirror it doesn't make my figure look odd, Grace zips up the back for me, I also wear a pair of heels.

I make sure I have my guns, I strap one to my thigh and the other I'll keep in my car then put it in my purse with my BPB badge.

I put my hair into a pony tail and several hair clips to keep my hair in place, lastly, I apply some lipstick and head down to Grace and Lexie.

"Well how do I look?" I ask them both, but all they do is stare. "Do I look that bad, I should have spent more time on my hair."

"No, you look stunning." Grace finally says.

"Yep, you look like a movie star." Lexie adds.

Grace approaches me and fixes a piece of my hair and says, "There."

"Okay, well here's the plan. Lexie I'm taking you back to your mum she's waiting for you, I texted her before. Grace you'll be here on your own for a few hours, Megan's number is on the fridge if you can't get hold of me."

"So, I can stay up late if you're not here?"

"If you want you haven't got school tomorrow." Grace looks at me surprised.

Grace hugs me and then like I told her locks the door so that she's safe.

On the way to Roxy's, Lexie tells me about one of the books I bought her which sounds interesting, so I ask her once she's read it if I could borrow it which she says of course.

"Lexie, you know Roxy cares about you a lot." Lexie nods. "It's just, it's probably not my place, but you scare her and me, but you really scare her by not taking your injections when you're meant to and she's always working when she just really would rather be with you." She doesn't say anything, so I don't add anything.

Lexie stays quiet for the rest of the journey, I get out the car and take her to the front door, Roxy answers.

Lexie hugs me, which is a first, then she drops her bags in the hallway and hugs Roxy for a long while.

Roxy looks at me, then says to Lexie, "Go get into your pyjamas and then we'll watch a film if you want?"

"Yeah, I'd like that." Lexie says giving her a big smile and runs up the stairs.

Roxy steps outside and closes the door over slightly, "What happened?" She asks meaning about Lexie, then adds, "And why you all dressed up? You look beautiful by the way."

"Thanks, and we had a little chat on the way here and I've got to go to a job, a charity gala."

"Well, I'll let you get going." We hug and then I climb back into the car.

Another expensive house with even a guard house at the beginning of the drive.

A man in his early forties maybe climbs into the front passenger seat.

"You know where you're going?" He asks with a hint of annoyance.

"Yes." I say sternly.

I follow the sat navigation on the centre console, the gala building has large pillars and an impressive fountain outside.

I hand my keys to a man who gives me a ticket with a number on.

Showing my BPB badge to a guard and giving our names they allow us in.

The doors are opened, and the many voices seep out.

Well everyone in hear is wearing expensive jewellery, I doubt anyone in here will start shooting.

There's many speeches and many people flashing oversized checks with many zeroes on.

Only one man with a noticeable scar on his cheek keeps catching my eye. After returning from the bathroom I catch him speaking to my client.

"What did he want?" I ask.

"He was asking odd questions."

"Like?" I ask reaching into my purse for my gun, which is in time, I watch the scarred man reach into his jacket and pulls out a long-barrelled gun.

"Get down!" I grab my clients head and make him bend over so he's a harder target.

Everyone begins to scream and begin to run, I can't get a clear shot, and everyone is pushing him to the front door.

Keeping my clients head down I half pull, half drag him to the back entrance.

I done my research and that's where the cars are parked, I can't run in these damn heels.

There's the man who took my car, he's frozen to the spot, gunshots are going off inside the building must be the BPB security.

"Where's my keys?" I ask but he looks at me blankly.

I move him away from the desk he's standing at, rooting through the draws I find a bunch of keys. I find mine as it has a pink ribbon on, Grace put it there as I kept losing them and it's quite hard to miss the pink ribbon.

I look over my shoulder and see the scarred man, I shoot at him. He takes cover.

I take the gun from my thigh and begin to suppress him while heading for the car.

Then I stop behind a car as I see movement out of the corner of my eye, I go to turn, but the glass from the cars shatter around me.

How many are there.

He must be reloading as the shattering glass has ceased. I pop my head up over the cars bonnet, his guns jammed, I slow my heaving chest take my aim and fire.

I hit him in the head, he falls to the floor.

We move quickly and climb into my car, he takes the front passenger seat again.

As soon as I'm in I speed off heading for the exit, that's when I notice the BPB security in formation, but I don't know who's enemy, so I don't stop they dive out the way as I drive past them.

I call Megan through the car.

"You heard?"

"Yes." Megan says.

"Where am I going? I have the client, he's safe."

"I'll put it on your GPS, there will be a response team waiting, then that's you done."

"Okay, thanks."

The GPS changes and shouts, "Keep left."

I keep my gun in my lap just in case, good job as well as he goes to put a hand on my knee, I pick up the gun and point it at him, while keeping the car straight.

"What are you doing? You won't shoot me, you just saved my life." He says in an uncertain voice.

"Would you like to test that theory?" I ask calmly.

"But I'm one of the biggest contributors to the BPB." He says more trying to reassure himself that I wouldn't shoot him.

"Then I'll shoot you twice, one for attempting something, the other to make sure you keep contributing, a third if you refuse to keep contributing. You get the point."

"They said you was the best." I think he means as I'm holding a gun steadily and driving the car.

"The best or you mean the only woman?"

"Both." He admits.

He seems to have got the point that I'm not interested, so I place the gun back in my lap.

We make it to the safehouse, the response team hasn't arrived yet.

"Hope that man finds you." The client mumbles, I think he's drunk.

"What?" I snap, he doesn't say anything. "What was that man asking you?"

"About you, where was you? Had I seen any weapons, it was quite odd."

"You don't tell anyone this!" I warn.

"Or what?" He says.

"Or I'll do a better job at killing you, do you understand?"

"Yes." He says like a child being told off.

Several black cars approach, I use the cars in built speaker.

"Show your badges." I say into the transmitter which sends my voice outside the car.

The man in charge holds it up to my window, good enough I lower the window.

"You've got glass in your hair ma'am." The BPB agent says.

"Oh yeah, are we done here. Can I go?"

The agent watches the client get into his car.

"Yes, have a good night ma'am."

"You too."

I drive back bare footed, my heels where hurting me.

Stepping into the house I shout, "Grace." No answer, it is late she must be asleep.

I find her on my bed wearing one of my skirts and one of my tops, by the look of all my clothes scattered on the floor she must have been trying them on.

The laptop on my bed is still open, I go to close it and notice someone's face illuminated by their own laptop on the other end.

Who is it? I look closer and make out the face, it's Lexie. I close the laptop and put it away.

I fix Graces skirt and gently lift her up, so I can put her under the duvet, so she doesn't get cold.

Then I go take a long hot bath and get the glass and dirt out my hair, once I have changed into my pyjamas I climb into bed next to Grace.

32 HOSPITAL

I wake the next day and as usual Grace isn't there and all the clothes on the floor have been put away.

I find Grace wearing just overalls.

"You know you're meant to where more clothes with them overalls, I can't allow you to go out like that."

"I didn't want to get paint on any of my clothes, it's easier to get off this."

"Oh, yeah sorry, in your draw there's covers start covering your things and I'll be in soon to help."

I eat breakfast quickly, then change into an old pair of jeans and a top and put my hair in a messy bun.

We paint the room, stopping only for lunch. We are both covered in paint, me more so as I accidently dropped some on Grace who took it that I did it on purpose and began to flick paint on me, resulting in a paint fight.

Standing back when finished we admire our work, it looks almost professional the dark red with hints of ocean blue Graces two favourite colours.

"Well go get washed and I'll order some food, you will have to sleep in my room tonight while it dries." Like she's going sleep anywhere else, she's still sleeping in my bed ugh.

Grace tells me what she wants and goes to get washed.

A few weeks pass without incident and then on my way to the safehouse for my lunch I get a dreadful call.

"Hello, are you Helena, Graces guardian?"

"Yes."

"We tried to call you, Grace is fine, but she's at the hospital."

I've already turned the car around and heading for the only children's hospital in the area.

"What happened?"

"Grace fell in P.E and bashed her head and blacked out for a second." She tells me the hospital and I hang up and call Megan.

"I heard," Megan says. "They called me, but I tried to call you, I don't want you to panic but we have chatter on the police scanners."

"What sort of chatter?"

"There's multiple reports of dirt bikes, all black, heading to the hospital, I've dispatched BPB agents, but they are far out."

I speed up, driving faster than I've ever dared to drive.

I realise that I haven't hung up the phone as Megan's voice says, "There's two police officers on motorbikes having their lunch they are offering to escort you, they are at the next junction."

"Well, I'm not slowing down." It would help a straight drive instead of weaving in and out of the traffic.

As I approach the next junction I see their flashing blue lights before I see them. They've closed the junction stopping traffic either side. I fly past sending debris into the air.

Eventually they catch up and overtake me, the cars part down the middle.

I look into my rear-view mirror, there's one of them, a bike, all black, catching up.

I wait until the person on the bike is looking at me, I swerve the car at them, but they pull on the brakes in time.

Again, I look in the rear-view mirror, they pull out a gun. No, you don't know one's ever shot at my car yet.

I press hard on the brakes as they try to swerve out the way they struggle and manage to get out the way of my car but fall to the ground and a car in the other lane clips them.

"There's a helicopter, landing on the roof all black, you may want to hurry." Megan says.

As I approach the hospital I hear gunfire, upon slowing down the police motorbikes slows and opens their visor.

"Sorry ma'am this is all we can go we don't have guns."

"That's okay, thanks for the escort."

The entrance to the car park is not accessible due to the many dumped cars.

I go on foot to the source of the shooting.

There's dumped bikes, but confusingly there's two sets, both sets firing at each other, taking cover behind the parked cars.

Who do I shoot at? Are they both here to hurt or capture Grace or me. Or is one set here to help but why are they both wearing the same outfits, and both have the same bikes.

Then I notice the helicopter, whoever was in it will be inside.

I decide to leave them to it, I'll deal with whoever attempts to come in the hospital.

I find a receptionist who seems to be not bothered by the gunfire outside, they inform me what ward Grace is on.

I get to the corridor where Graces ward is located and freeze, quickly taking out my guns, both.

There's three of them in the same black outfits two holding guns either side of a man who they seem to be loyal to.

"Helena." The man in the middle says holding up his hands. "Go see Grace I'll secure the corridor."

Is it a trap. I walk towards them cautiously to the doors behind them, I keep my guns aimed on each one and only holster them when the doors to the ward are closed behind me.

The nurse on the ward leads me to her bed.

Grace is sitting upright, I throw myself at her hugging her tightly and kissing her on the head.

"You're choking me." Grace manages to say.

"Oh, sorry." I say loosening my grip, but still hugging her. Eventually I sit in a chair at her bedside.

"Why are you crying?" Grace asks me, and I feel a hot tear fall down my cheek.

I wipe the tears away.

"I thought you was seriously injured."

"Well, I do have a cut on my head and I scared the teachers and Lexie, oh, can you phone her?"

I take out my phone and call Lexie.

"Here, you can still talk?" She looks at me like of course.

"I'll be back in a second." The nurse lets me out.

I don't draw my weapon, but I keep my hand on one of them just in case.

The two soldiers are stationed at either end of the corridor. But the man in charge is nowhere to be seen.

"He's in there ma'am." One of the soldiers says realising I'm looking for him.

I head into the office that he's pointing at. I notice his large belly not allowing him to sit properly behind the desk.

"Hello." He says.

"Hello." I say to him.

"The soldiers are dead or have fled."

"What's your name?"

"My name is not important, the Grand Master sent me from the order."

"And who were the soldiers?" I ask.

"They are from a different faction within the Templar order." That's when I notice his Templar ring. "They don't like you being a General, amongst other things."

"Why?"

"It's the Grand Masters place to tell you the inner workings of the order. Simplified you're a General meaning head of your faction."

"My faction? But I don't even know much about the order."

"All I can say is get your faction in order."

"It's just me."

"I know that." He says sounding annoyed. "I mean start hiring, you need to hire to have a faction, so things like today can't happen."

"You mean I need soldiers, guards?"

"Yes, after today, BPB won't give you guards, they'll fear you."

"But I don't have the finances to hire as many people as you're suggesting."

"I'll inform the Grand Master, you are a part of an old secret organisation usually that means each faction General has large amounts of wealth, as it is past down to each generation. You will probably get a few million to start hiring, but you'll need to start making your own money."

"How?"

"I don't know, buy houses, restaurants."

"What am I going to do in the meantime?"

"The two soldiers out there are my best, they will guard you and Grace, they will be under your command but report to me."

I sit back in the chair with a lot to think about.

"Well I have to thank you and I need to get back to Grace."

He nods.

I head back to the ward. Grace seems to be back to her normal self.

"Megan called, she said you need to call her back."

"Ok, is Lexie okay?"

"Yeah, she said she was worried."

A nurse informs me they are doing a few more checks on Grace, so I call Megan.

Megan tells me what the General in the office has already told me, she tried her best to get us guards, but the BPB are, like the General said scared and confused as are their shareholders which is never a good sign, Megan also told me that we need to meet which I agree.

"Grace can go home now, just check in on her in the night to make sure she's okay."

The nurse hands me some painkillers in case Grace needs them and a fresh bandage if she needs it when I take her current one-off tomorrow.

Grace is still in her P.E kit, her bag with her clothes in is next to her bed.

I put my blazer over her and take her bag. The two soldiers are outside the ward.

"Where's your General?"

"Gone."

"Very well, I'm going home."

Grace can walk but she holds my hand tightly.

The two soldiers jump onto their dirt bikes and follow close behind.

33 COTTAGE

The following day, Once I've seen to Graces head wound, I get a phone call, an odd one.

"Hello, this is detective O'Hare. Is this Helena?"

"It is."

"A Sergeant told me you have a key to a cottage in Conwy?"

"Uh, yeah, I think I still have it. I don't intend to use it though, it's not mine."

"Well, you need to meet me there, it's yours now, we are tracking owners who haven't returned, and they haven't returned we found them dead, killed by the storm a closed case. We have no one to pass the cottage to, no friends or family, as we were told you have a key we are happy to sign it over to you."

"Oh, well can I get back to you, to arrange when I can meet you?"

"Yes, that's fine, I'm here in the police station in Conwy."

"Okay, well I'll get back to you."

Grace takes the day off and so do I, oddly Megan doesn't say no, although she does insist again that we need to meet in person when I can.

I receive a handwritten letter, that's signed by the Grand Master and has a Templar seal.

'You will receive funds to get your faction in order, any soldiers need to understand if the UK goes to war so do they, we are a splinter army. We just send our soldiers covertly to do missions until war is called.' It read.

The same week Roxy informs me Graces parents' house sold for two hundred and fifty thousand and I'll receive the money in the separate bank account that I opened as it's going to Grace when she turns eighteen.

When I tell Grace this she just keeps telling me that she doesn't want it, she looks at me angrily as if I shouldn't even be suggesting it, but I don't care Grace is having the money.

"You finish for full term for two weeks on Friday, don't you?" I ask Grace who's lying on her stomach reading.

"Yes." Her legs stop fidgeting in the air. "Why?"

"Would you like to go on holiday, camping?"

Grace hesitates, "Yeah, I'd like that." She says smiling and her legs continue to fidget in the air. Without looking up from her book she adds, "It might be cold."

"It's always cold these days."

"And," she adds. "Isn't it your birthday as well one of them weeks?"

"Um," I say trying to remember what month it is. "Oh, yeah how did you know?"

"Roxy told me, and I saw it on your driving license."

I go to work just waiting for Friday, Grace informs me on the Tuesday that Lexie was saying she'd like to come which means I should call Roxy.

"Grace told me, that Lexie told her, that she'd like to join us on holiday camping for one week, when they are off." I say to Roxy.

"Lexie did mention it, I've been meaning to call we seem to meet only on the weekends recently with work giving me more overtime."

"But the weekends are still fun." I add.

"True, true." She says. "Can you take Lexie for the two weeks?"

"Two? I can, but I was going to surprise Grace on Friday by picking her up from school early."

"Well I don't mind you taking Lexie out early, it wouldn't have been fair anyway Grace and Lexie are in each other's pockets."

"You mean like we were?" I say.

"Yep, we will keep this a secret if we can, I may be able to get one day off if I do I'll come see you all."

The days seem to slow as they always seem to when you're waiting for something exciting.

Finally, the day comes, Roxy keeps telling me to make sure Lexie takes her injections, which I keep telling her I obviously will, and I will make sure nothing happens to her.

I drop them both off, Grace kept asking me if Lexie could come, I kept saying we'll see.

Then I head home packing everything I'll need including the new tent I bought and my new camping gear and packing clothes for Grace mainly practical outfits and her favourites which include some of my clothes, including my sweater which are oversized on her. I pack a few sweat shirts just in case it's super cold.

Next, I head to Roxy's and let myself in as she gave me a key in case of emergency.

Roxy isn't in as she's in work.

I head to the kitchen, where there's a padded bag with a note.

'Two weeks' worth of injections and a few spare ones, be careful with them. Also, there's a gym bag in my room for Lexie's clothes.'

I open the bag there's bottles and needles. I zip the bag back up and head up the stairs and find the gym bag, then head to Lexie's room.

Lexie's room is like Graces, messy, clothes all over the floor and several charges on the bed and on the desk next to a laptop a spilled box of glitter.

I put the charger which has a phone manufactures symbol on in the bag and then begin to pack two weeks' worth of clothes, the bag now nearly bursting at the seams, I go outside and place both the padded bag and gym bag in the boot.

Before I head back to the school, I call the detective O'Hare informing him that I'll be able to meet, he says it's fine and for me to just head to the police station and ask for him.

I'm also meeting Megan at the cottage to speak about my future at BPB, but I have a plan.

When I told the soldiers, I was going camping in a weeks' time they seemed extremely happy.

I get back to the school and wait in the reception area.

"I'm here to pick up Grace and Lexie, I already got permission off the headmaster." I say to the receptionist.

"Oh, yes." The receptionist says looking down at a list. "Lexie's guardian also called us, wait here I'll go get them."

I spot Grace and Lexie, Graces face lights up when she sees me and speeds up giving me a big hug.

"What are you doing here?" Grace asks still with a big smile.

"We're going on holiday."

"Including Lexie?" Grace asks.

"Yep." Lexie's face now lights up. "I'll explain in the car."

"I need to change, and I need to get my injections." Lexie says with a hint of panic as she climbs into the car.

"It's okay, I've got everything." I say calming her.

Then I explain and when we get to Conwy I find the police station; the girls wait in the car.

I enter the police station it has that feeling, like the building has stood for many years and has never changed.

"I'm here to see detective O'Hare."

"Wait here."

There's nowhere to wait, I'm in a narrow corridor so I just linger.

"You are Helena?" A man asks. I thought it was a woman on the phone as the voice was high pitched.

"Yes, we talked on the phone about the cottage."

"Ah, yes, follow me, this way."

We walk through narrow corridors; the station seems small and not busy. Peering into some rooms I notice police officers sitting idly.

"Afternoon Henry." Detective O'Hare says to another detective in the room.

"Oh, hello. Want a cake?"

"No thanks." O'Hare says. I take a seat opposite him. He rifles through a bunch of paperwork with his tongue sticking out in concentration. "Here it is, do you have ID on you?"

I place my driving license and my agent badge.

He looks at the agent badge stopping whatever he was doing.

"I've only ever seen one of these before." He says. "You can carry guns, can't you? Can I see?" He adds sounding excited.

I unzip my jacket and show him one, making sure he doesn't touch it.

"Cool, I always wanted to join the matrix, you know the gun squad in the police, decided to be a detective instead. Anyway, I will fill in the paperwork."

He does and makes me sign then leaves and brings back my copy in case anyone contests it, I also show him the key, so he can confirm the Sergeants story.

"Well good luck." I shake his hand and pocket the paperwork and leave; the two guards smile and wave at me then begin to put on their helmets.

The cottage is a two-minute drive if that as it is also housed within the villages castle walls that once stood to stop invaders.

On approach I look at the door and windows, seems to be intact so no one has broken in.

"You own a cottage?" Lexie asks.

"I do now, remember it Grace?"

Grace nods and we head in.

34 AMBITIOUS PLANS

It's as I remember it, cosy and small. The small room that we enter which has a TV, couch, log burner and then the stairs leading to the bathroom and two bedrooms.

"Go get changed, I'll see if I can find some food." I hand Lexie and Grace their bags, while they do I go check the back door and find that it's secure.

The kitchen has no food, luckily the shops are a three-minute walk.

We go for a walk together picking up food then we walk down to the harbour and then go for a walk on the walls, which eventually takes us back to the cottage, where we sit on the floor next to the log fire all cosy under a blanket.

The next day I go to check my bank account, what? Good job there's no line behind me as I'm staring at the zeroes.

"Grace come here please." Grace and Lexie appear to the left and right of me. "How many zeroes are there?"

"Six." Grace says after tracing them on the screen with her fingers. "Where did you get that money from?"

"I'll tell you back at the cottage." I say and take out some money, still in shock as I didn't realise the order would send me so much money like it's loose change.

We decide today that we will go into the castle as we didn't see much of it that one time when we went there, and Lexie hasn't ever been in there.

After that we head to the harbour as they want to do crabbing as they noticed people doing it, sitting on the harbour wall, lowering their lines and hooks into the water then pulling it up with crabs hanging on.

The day after I have a meeting with Megan, we sit in the kitchen and I close the door over.

"Want a drink of tea?" I ask.

"Yes please."

I make tea while Megan begins to pull out a bunch of paperwork.

"BPB are scared especially after what happened at the hospital and they know you have your own guards and they don't know where they are from."

"Well, what are my options? You said I need to be there for a year, I have plans after a year, but I need to do those plans now."

"Oh, what plans? It might help with my suggestion." Megan says blowing on her tea, then takes a sip.

"Ok, you know the order, where I'm a General that also means I'm a faction leader. I want to create my own business, I was wondering would you leave BPB to help me?"

"You can start your own business now, on paper you work for a splinter army, that means the splinter army have the same interests as the government. Meaning the government is happy for you to leave BPB." She informs me.

"And would you join me? I'm thinking about giving people shares, for now I can pay you right away to help me set it up."

"I'd be delighted, BPB aren't happy with me either they think I've been badly advising you. We will need a person who knows business law."

"My friend Roxy can do that, she's really good her company keep making her do overtime, she'll also have shares in the company. I'm meeting her tomorrow."

"What will the company do?" Megan asks putting down her tea cup.

"The plan is, at first a security company, then houses, restaurants anything that will generate a lot of money. I want to build an empire." I say proudly.

"Very ambitious, I like it. I can help with the security I can bring over some clients, you just need security personnel."

"I have some in mind. Can you get the phone numbers of a Sergeant Crater and a Lieutenant George?"

"I will get you the numbers by tomorrow. Boss." She says the last part with a smile.

"Don't forget to call Roxy, I need you to work on getting the company official. I will text you her number when and if she agrees to join."

We shake hands and I pull her into a hug, if we are going to be in business together we should be on hugging terms.

The following day Roxy arrives, she did after all manage to get two days off.

Again, I close the door over and tell her my plan Roxy seems pleased with it.

"I'll need a week, the company makes me work too much, but I can't leave them just yet. They have a big problem that needs sorting."

"That's fine, after a week I will need your help on making the company official."

After discussing business, we go to the cinema which is close by, then to a pizza restaurant.

We get back late after going for a drive in the dark down country lanes, animal's eyes reflect the light beams from the cars headlights.

The drive would be nice and quiet if it wasn't for the guards on their motorbikes.

There's only two beds so Roxy and I share one and the girls share the other.

The next day we decide to have a lazy day, we get up late and wander around the shops, buying the girls many sweets, which keeps them quiet for a few hours.

Also buying them most of their camping gear, Grace buys a pink waterproof jacket, at least I'll be able to spot her a mile away.

Roxy leaves that night, after saying goodbye to Lexie and says that she'll see her next Saturday.

35 BIRTHDAY

We make sure everything is packed back into the car, then set off for the campsite in Snowdonia.

When we arrive, we put the tent up, the farmer comes over and we pay. I give extra.

After the tents up and the pegs are secure, that's when I take in the beauty of our surroundings.

We are in a valley, several mountains surround us, and a river runs next to the campsite, it even has a small stony shore that acts like a beach.

Taking our shoes off, we walk into the water instantly realising it was a bad idea as the water is icy cold.

But Grace and Lexie have fun splashing water at each other.

I'm sitting on the river shore throwing stones into the water when one of the guard's approaches.

"Ma'am a note arrived."

"How? We're in the middle of nowhere."

"We have an eagle ma'am."

"Oh, you'll have to tell me how that works when I'm back home." I say as I'm interested.

"Yes, ma'am."

I pull apart the seal it reads:

To Helena

I hope the money is enough, it should be if you use it wisely. Talking of being wise, put one million into a separate bank account and send these four men a message.

Hickman.

Gustav.

David.

Fenston.

The message must include your name, the bank numbers and this sentence, the ship sails under the sea but only at night. Tell no one.

P.S the address to send the letter to is on the back.

As I go to make dinner on the gas bottle, Lexie stops me.

"Can you help me?" Lexie asks holding her injection.

"What do you need me to do?" I ask putting down a box of matches and wiping my palms on my pants.

Lexie hands me the injection, sits in a camping chair and rolls up the leg of her pants revealing her thigh.

"I'd normally do it myself but I'm feeling weak today, I only ask others when I'm having a bad day."

Lexie points where it needs to go, and I gently put it in her thigh and press the plunger.

Once I finish doing that and fussing over Lexie I begin to make dinner, then the girls put on their pyjama tops, but it's getting cold, so I give them both one of my jumpers and we climb into the tent bumping into each other as we struggle into our sleeping bags under one torch.

I throw a large blanket over all of us.

In the morning I'm woken by the sunrise, the suns low on the horizon, the sun's rays gently touching the tent warming the inside.

I look left and right to find both Lexie and Grace asleep, they look peaceful in their sleepy dreamy state. I take a picture, so I can send it to Roxy show how peaceful her adopted daughter looks. Grace is always taking pictures of me when I am unawares so a little bit of payback.

I climb out my sleeping bag, carefully making sure not to wake them, I put on my boots and quietly unzip the tent and climb outside.

The fresh air is refreshing, and the valley is so peaceful and quiet.

I wave to the two guards who are already wide awake, both squatting over a pot of tea probably.

After stretching my legs, I go to wash my face in the washing facilities which is over the other side of the field, I probably should have put the tent closer, but the walk over there is relaxing.

When back, I take out a chair and read my book out the corner of my eye I catch a guard approaching.

"Tea Ma'am?" He asks holding out a mug.

I take it saying, "Thanks."

"Morning." Grace says as she stretches while yawning and sits on the grass to put her shoes on.

"Morning." I say. "I got you back." I add holding out the phone.

"Oh." Grace says. "It's only fair." It's the picture of her asleep, she stands up and hands me the phone back.

"You mean fair because of all the pictures you have of me asleep, it can be seen as creepy you know."

Grace shrugs and begins to walk across the field.

Lexie appears next, who also does a big stretch and yawns with a, "Morning."

"Morning, are you feeling better today?"

Lexie nods and also begins to walk across the field.

I make bacon it's ready when they both come back together.

"What are we going to do today?" Grace asks as she bites into her bacon sandwich.

"If you want we can go for a walk up a mountain? I have a picnic in the car."

They both nod in approval as their mouths are full.

While they get dressed I go to wash the dishes.

I attach a silencer to my weapon as I get to the wash basin, there's one man running across a field, he has a sniper rifle in both arms. I wait until he points it at me to confirm he is here to hurt me, then I make sure no other camper is watching as I take aim and fire, he drops into the field, the grass hiding him from view.

I wait a few seconds he doesn't get up, so I holster my weapon and quickly wash the dishes.

When I get back I tell the guards what happened, one of them goes to clean it up the other follows us to a mountain.

Do I continue our holiday is the question, could he have been working alone like the guards suggested?

I decide to continue our holiday; the guards are more alert now and they are more than capable.

We go for a walk and decide to have a picnic by a lake, I place a picnic blanket on the floor and place the food on it, so everyone can eat what they want.

I pull out my gun quickly and fire at something moving in the grass.

It was a snake, I haven't seen a snake in the wild before. I feel ashamed though I could have easily just shot a dog by accident. I need to be more careful.

"Cool your reactions were amazing, I can't wait to tell Roxy." Lexie says.

"No, don't tell your mother." I shout a little too quickly, both look at me with a surprised expression.

"Why?" Lexie asks.

"Because she'll never let me see you again, never mind take you on holiday."

Lexie looks at me with an understanding that she won't tell Roxy.

The next day I'm surprised to see Grace and Lexie are not in their sleeping bags, but the extra room allows me to have a big stretch.

I put on my boots and step outside.

"Surprise." Both say, Grace holding a cupcake.

"I've also got the guards making breakfast." Grace says, she walks to the boot of the car and starts rooting around and brings back a bag.

Grace and Lexie both root through the bag pulling out several wrapped parcels.

"How did you hide these from me?" I ask genuinely surprised.

"Well." Grace begins, she tells me how she asked if Roxy could buy several items for her as Grace knows I check my bank statements whenever she borrows my card. Grace said she asked Roxy to take it from her inheritance, but Grace thought she was lying when she said ok.

Then Roxy brought them with her when she came to the cottage and Lexie and Grace hid it in the boot amongst the camping gear.

Also, she hid the cupcake in multiple napkins, then wrapped her jumper around it and apparently, I nearly found it when I was getting their clothes for them.

I look at the cake it does have a squashed look to it, but it does look nice.

Before they hand me presents they tell me to eat the cake, I can't eat the cake in front of two children. After them saying no several times, they finally agree to help me eat it if I have the biggest piece, as it is my birthday.

It was a super tasty cake.

Then I open presents that have been excellently wrapped. Off Grace I receive a locket, gold with several diamonds set into it, in the shape of a heart. I open the locket to find, on one side a picture of Grace and on the other side a picture of me and Grace.

"Maybe it's a bit much, giving you a picture of me." Grace says as she scrunches up her face as if it was a silly idea.

"No, it's, it's the best thing I own." Grace smiles. "Help me."

Grace lifts my pony tail, puts it around my neck and closes the clasp. The locket lies heavily on my chest, more heavily because of its worth to me.

Grace also hands me three more packages.

"You always ask me for advice on clothes, so I hope you didn't mind me buying clothes for you."

"No, I don't mind, I would have, like you said asked for your advice anyway."

"Well one of them is questionable, meaning I'm unsure about." Grace adds which makes me hope that it's not anything that will look odd.

One is a top that will show off my shoulders and collarbones as Grace said it's a good feature of mine, the second package is a white backless dress, then I open the last which must be the questionable one.

It's a grey crop top with a flannel shirt.

"Why questionable?" I ask looking at it, it looks perfectly fine.

"Well I've never seen you choose to show off your stomach, that's why I got the tartan shirt as well, so you can fasten it up if you don't like it."

"Well I'll put it on in a second, see how it looks."

"Grace told me you like running, so I got you this." Lexie hands me a present, I open it. It's a fitness tracker that goes around my wrist and with the help of the girls we manage to get it to connect to my phone.

There's also a birthday card from Roxy and Lexie with several shopping vouches.

I give them both hugs and lots of thanks.

I change into my crop top, which shows my stomach, it's quite chilly, so I'm thankful for the flannel shirt.

Lexie touches my stomach which causes me to jump, I didn't realise until I felt her cold fingers. She says sorry and then asks me if I have a fitness routine. Which I do have one as I need to keep fit for my job.

The guards come over with breakfast and again with much persuasion I get them to join us for breakfast.

36 TEMPLAR GIFT

We are all in pain from the long walk up the mountain which means we all decide for an easier walk in Betws, a riverside walk to a waterfall.

Along the way we decide to stop near the water's edge and eat our food we bought from the bakery.

"Helena." Grace says to get my attention. I feel a serious conversation happening.

"What's up?" I ask finishing a cake.

"We heard in the cottage you are starting a business, I know you don't need money. But I don't want my inheritance, I was thinking if I give you it then I can get some shares in your company and if you make a success of it, which I know you will, then any profits I make off my shares. I can say I made that money."

Hmm, I'm talking to a twelve-year-old nearly thirteen about business, sometimes I forget her age.

I must admit her plan is a good one as she, for some reason doesn't want the money, if the company failed I could just make sure she got the exact amount back.

And if the company succeeded she would make more than two hundred and fifty thousand meaning she would be set for life, plus when she's old enough I'd be able to talk to her about business.

Either way fail or not I think Grace will be a formidable business woman.

"Helena, Grace and friends." I say and Graces face lights up.   .

"So that's a yes?" Grace asks excitingly.

"I'll think about it, but we have to ask Roxy if it's legally possible."

I can tell Grace is trying to keep in her excitement as she kicks her legs splashing water at Lexie, who's knee deep in the river splashing water at Grace in return.

I throw them a towel and then we keep on walking next to the river.

Eventually we come across a bridge that goes over the river, we can hear it now, the great thundering noise coming from in front of us.

When we start to cross the bridge we spot it, water cascading, water rushing so fast I couldn't compare the speed to anything.

Lexie, Grace and I, take a picture of us all with the waterfall behind. Lexie uses my phone to send the picture to Roxy.

On the way back, we take a different route along the pavement into the village.

A car screeches to a stop next to me, I hear the click of the safety being turned off from the guards behind me.

A man jumps out the green military vehicle, salutes me and hands me a letter.

People are staring, I salute back, he jumps back into the vehicle and off it goes.

It reads:

Happy birthday, before you leave the area I'd like you to check out a cave, we only just deciphered a note the maps on a separate page. I know you have company therefore it's not dangerous whatever you find is yours.

The Grand Master.

"I guess we're going treasure hunting."

We don't need to get in the car. With the two guards we all come to a decision that the caves close by. We head on a path up a mountain trail.

Stopping to look at the map we decide that we need to go off the trail and into the forest, the towering trees feel like they're watching us.

The forest gets us lost, eventually we spot it. Between two rocks we notice a dark entrance, a guard hands me a torch.

I go in first, the girls seem to stick close to my back as we begin to enter the mysterious pitch-black cave.

A long tunnel takes us to a cavernous section.

On the back of the map there's a cave, the same size as this one an X in the corner, yep an X like a treasure map.

The guards go to dig but I take a spade off one of them and help.

We hear a thud and we must clear the rest of the dirt with our hands, then we climb out of the hole with a large chest.

Hitting the lock with the spade it doesn't budge.

"Put your hands over your ears." I say to the girls, while taking out my gun and fire at the lock which falls to the floor.

I open it while working my jaw to get sound back into my ears. Inside there's several scrolls which I move aside carefully as they look old and delicate.

Revealing a large statue or bust, a woman's head ending at her chest, it's in perfect condition, who it is though I have no idea.

Next to the bust a sword, I pull it out expecting the blade to be rusty but nope it looks brand new and still got a sharp edge, on the hilt a large red Templar insignia.

"Why would the blade not be rusted?" I ask the guards.

One shrugs and adds, "Don't know Ma'am."

Grace and Lexie help me carry the chest out while the guards keep watch.

When we get to the car, I check for any nearby antique shops and I find one close by. I wrap the sword in one of the girl's towels.

"Come on, we are going to an antique shop."

The antique shop looks more like someone's home in a cottage. The guards luckily wait outside as inside it's cramped with many antiques.

An old looking man wearing thin glasses comes out the back.

"Hello dears, want to buy anything?"

"No," I say. "I was wondering if you could look at this."

I unwrap the sword, the old man picks it up by the hilt and in the other hand holds a magnifying glass.

"Brand new blade, just made." But then he suddenly stops on the hilt. "But the paint looks old, maybe a hundred years as if from the…" He looks up at me. "Where did you get this?"

"I can't say specifically. Close by."

"I thought so, read this." He turns around and takes a dusty book off the shelf. "I write down all stories I hear about local legends or mysteries this is my favourite."

I read: A local templar had a sword made from a fallen star, thought to be a rare metal that would never rust, never break and never lose its edge.

"You think…" I go to ask but he starts nodding and smiling.

"You found it."

"What's its value?"

"If you got the metal confirmed, then hundreds of thousands of pounds, old families would bid against each other." He stops now staring at my hand. "You, you're." He continues to babble.

I think it's time to leave, I bundle up the sword in my arms and hurry out.

All I can think of is the sword. We find a restaurant to eat, then head back to the tent for our last night. The girls show me their talent in gymnastics, Grace apparently taught Lexie how to do the splits as she had difficulty and in return Lexie showed Grace how to keep balance when doing continuous cartwheels which is impressive.

The morning I receive a note from the Grand Master:

Your ceremonial sword, send the scrolls to me. I'll have people look at them. I will also send someone to look at the bust but it's yours.

We pack away the tent and head to Roxy's, we don't stop. I drop Lexie off who gives me a big hug and thanks me for the holiday.

Having a quick word with Roxy she tells me she has now quit her job, we plan to celebrate when the company is officially created.

We hug twice as we are both are extremely happy and excited for the future, then I head home and take a bath.

37 RECRUITMENT

The next day is busy, I send a letter to these four people and head to a bank to transfer one million to a separate account, then back home to call the Sergeant and the Lieutenant.

If I wasn't busy enough the Sergeant jumps at the invitation he's coming tonight, the Lieutenant has family, so he said he'll have to get back to me.

And on top of that the Grand Master has sent a man who's wearing an expensive suit to look at the bust and the sword, he tells me to ignore him, he'll leave when he's done, and I'll receive a letter of his findings.

Grace complains about having to change out of her pyjamas, I tell her that she doesn't have to change, she looks at me as if to say don't be silly.

There's a great thud, thud on the door, it's the Sergeant Crater I met in Conwy, Megan found out where he could be contacted. He's wearing a suit and holding a cane, he steps into the house limping.

"The guards outside took the wine from me." He says.

"Sorry about that. They are just being careful." I offer him a beer.

"Where's your sister?" He asks which confuses me.

"Oh, Grace." I tell him the truth that Grace is now my adopted daughter.

"Makes sense why you would lie." He admits.

"So, you still work for the army?"

"No," he says sipping his beer and takes a seat on the couch. "Honourable discharge on medical grounds, in the hospital they couldn't fix my leg. I can walk without the cane, but it hurts."

"You don't have a job then?"

"No, are you offering?" He asks laughing as if it was a joke.

"Yes, actually." His smile fades, his face more stunned now. "Would you be willing to be in the military again?"

"I can't, my leg, I'd be a liability."

162

"Nonsense, can you still walk fast? Can you still drive? If you can't run are you good with a gun?"

"Yes but-"

"But nothing, I see you fit for duty in my army. I must make you aware if you accept you are aware as a splinter army if the UK goes to war only in a world war you'll be required to join, other wars it will be voluntary. Or up to the General me."

"I couldn't carry my gear if that happened."

"You'd be one of my Lieutenants, you can order someone to carry it. Besides the military thing is hazy and lines are blurred. You will mainly work for Helena, Grace and friends doing security work." He doesn't say anything. "Do you accept you don't have to accept now, I'll need an answer in a few days."

"Yes, I'll accept. Being stuck in the house all day is boring."

"Good, tomorrow I'll need you to gather soldiers if you can, people you trust I need security."

We talk some more and then eat, Grace is quiet all the while.

Crater seems happier, like he has a purpose again. When he leaves I feel tired. It's still tiring entertaining guests.

During the week I admit I'm bored, my duties at BPB have now ceased, so all I'm doing all day is ferrying Grace and Lexie to and from school. We have also decided to allow Grace to spend her money on shares, I must do it in front of a judge for legal reasons.

Lieutenant George is coming on Friday night, I have Lexie over for a sleepover with Grace, so again it will be busy.

Friday comes and again Roxy informs me that I need to check Lexie's blood sugar level.

The girls are upstairs when I hear a knock on the door.

I open the door to Lieutenant George, he's holding a small girl in his arms, the girl has some of his features, but the mother's eyes.

"I brought my daughter, I know I should have called to see if it was okay."

"No, it's fine. Come in out the cold." They enter. "And who are you?" I ask the girl who goes shy and turns her head into her father's chest.

"This is Riley." He says and starts tickling her, she starts giggling.

He tells me his wife is with their son at a football practice match, who insisted he wanted his mum there.

He also tells me he brought wine and again the guards have taken it, ugh I told them to stop taking things off guests.

George also tells me he is no longer a Lieutenant, under his wife's instruction and the realisation he was missing his children growing up he decided to leave.

"Would you like to be a Lieutenant again?" Excitement seems to flash in his eyes, then quickly fades. "You wouldn't be as busy, nine to five, until we get soldiers then on call, holidays anytime, extra holidays if things are ever to busy."

"There sounds like a catch." He says looking at me suspiciously.

I tell him about the world war issue which is most unlikely.

Riley comes down with Graces help to make sure she doesn't fall down the stairs as she has been in her room. Riley jumps up and sits on my lap and gives me a wide smile, no longer shy.

George is still quiet thinking it over.

"And I answer only to you?" He asks breaking the silence. I nod to him. "Okay, well I will talk to the wife before giving you an answer."

I say that's fine and can't help but smile.

We eat and chat for a while before there's a beep from outside, his wife is here to pick them up.

38 NEW BEGINNINGS

Next morning, I somehow wake up on a tiny part of my own bed, Grace and Lexie taking up the rest of it.

When they are ready, we climb into the car and head to the courts, Grace and Lexie are unaware.

"Why are you wearing a dress, you only usually do that when somethings happening?" Grace asks looking at me with suspicion.

"I don't need a reason to wear a dress."

I'm giving Lexie a four percent share in the company, so Roxy is meeting us there, Roxy is also getting eleven percent.

Everything goes smoothly and when Lexie and Roxy come out of the courtroom I receive a long hug from Lexie and to my surprise a kiss on the cheek. Her way of saying thank you.

We go for a celebratory lunch in a restaurant.

"So, when will I see profits from my investment?" Grace asks with a serious looking expression, then she bursts into laughter and we all join her. "But seriously what will you do with my money?"

"Well." I start then sip my drink. "Roxy is looking for an office in Liverpool, so we can work together instead of from home and if we use your money we can say you bought it."

"Would you like to go take a look at one? I have the keys." Roxy asks holding the keys up.

"Okay." I say, and we pay then hurry to the car.

We head to a skyscraper, well more of the tallest building in the city, which has underground car parking.

Then we take a lift to the top floor where Roxy takes a key to open the lift doors to an empty reception desk.

All the walls and doors are glass, several offices line the edges and a large office in the centre, with a large conference table in the middle.

"Come take a look at the view." Roxy says and takes us into a corner office.

We can see the liver birds atop the liver building and the cathedrals.

We all jump and shout in fright as a figure moves from behind a desk at a far office.

Then the woman moves her hair out her face and we realise its Megan.

Roxy tells me quickly that Megan has been staying in the offices we get when we get the free trials.

"Megan." I say as she enters our office. "You're sleeping at ours tonight, don't say no or I will have to take you by gunpoint." Megan bites her lip as she seemed to be about to protest.

"Well I need to finish my work." She says.

"Okay, but we expect you for dinner at four."

Megan nods in acceptance and asks, "The views amazing, isn't it?"

"Yes." I say. "So, can we buy it? It is in a good location and views to impress clients."

"Well," Roxy begins. "Megan and I can get the ball rolling, we have access to the company bank account. We can both see you at four, Lexie can go with you."

Lexie hugs Roxy then we leave.

I receive a phone call from George, he has accepted my offer, I now have two Lieutenants.

I also now have two new guards, meaning the old ones have went back to their faction leader with my thanks. My new guards are ex-SAS, I couldn't have hoped for better, they are friends of Craters.

Although they continually say that I should have more guards due to so many shareholders in one house.

Next week the company starts its first contracts, doing my old job, driving people around mainly.

I have parents evening tonight ugh, I know Grace would have done good.

I meet Grace at the school, she has been helping them prepare.

"My lips are dry." I say to Grace, for some reason I'm nervous, Grace hands me a stick. I take it, it must be lip balm.

It's not until I look at it after I've applied it that I realise it's a glitter one.

Grace looks at me smiling, I kiss her on the cheek to get her back. It leaves a glittery lip mark on her face.

Before we get to the first teacher, we are stopped by, I think the headmaster.

"I'm headmaster Mc Claggin, I was wondering if I can have a word?"

"Yeah, sure."

We head to his office, Grace sits on a chair outside.

"I was wondering if you'd accompany a class on a trip, I thought I might ask as it's Graces class and I know you would be sending the guards with them."

"Yes, I'd love to. Where are they going?"

"Excellent," he says clapping his hands together. "They are going hiking up Snowdon, a mountain in wales. The teacher takes a class up each year, I was wondering if you could give them a lesson in something?"

"Like what? I know how to use a compass, that's handy when hiking."

"Wonderful you can do that then, I take it you know how to put up a tent?"

"Yes."

"Good, good. My secretary can give you the details or Grace can I suppose." He stops and looks at me. "It was nice meeting you."

We shake hands and I leave.

39 SCHOOL TRIP

Then we head to the first teacher, who is Graces English teacher, who says Grace is doing exceptionally well, on track to getting good grades in a few years, when she sits her exams.

The rest of the teachers are the same with lots of praise for Grace. Most also say that they would like to see her participate more, maybe do some after school activities.

The only negative comments were that of Grace and Lexie often talk a little too much in most of their classes, Grace looks at me as if to I'm sorry.

I'll still have a word with her later, but if she's doing well I don't see the issue unless she is disrupting Lexie's learning.

The last one of the night her science teacher, oddly I notice mood change. Her shoulders drop.

We exchange introductions and then he begins.

"Well, Grace is doing ok, she does answer me back a lot."

"So does everyone." Grace mumbles under her breath.

"As I was saying, answers back, I also receive half completed homework when I know she's more than capable. Also walking around with that expensive bracelet on of hers. I mean you are a young parent, probably the youngest in the school, only natural for Grace to rebel, boundaries not properly set and all that."

"Stop, Joseph." I say his name and he looks at me as if he's been struck, as we're only meant to know their surnames. "Firstly, I'd support Grace if she wanted to wear a crown on her head although that would be a bit much. Secondly, would your wife Jenifer know how you treat your students?" His face completely shocked. "I thought she wouldn't and by your face, I guess she'd be horrified as doesn't your wife help at a charity for young parents who need help?" Again, his face increases more in panic now, trying to find words but finding none. "So, every teacher has praised

Grace on her achievements this far and praised me on my parenting this far. Therefore, I will make sure Grace tells me how you've changed. If you haven't I'll get the headmaster involved, got it?" He nods, I stand and hold out my hand to Grace. "Come on Grace we're leaving."

Grace takes my hand and we leave him there stuck to his seat.

"How did you know all those things about him?" Grace asks when we're in the car, applying more glitter lip balm.

"The headmaster allowed me to run checks on all teachers and staff employed by the school, due to safety reasons because you and Lexie are a part of a multimillion pound company."

"The company has made profit then?"

"Yep. We received three million from those four people on the stock market."

"So, how much profit do I receive?" Grace asks.

"Erm, I'm not good at math you'll have to ask Roxy." We sit in silence on the way home before my stomach rumbles. "Would you like a burger?" I ask as we're close to fast food and I'm quite hungry. Grace nods.

We go through the drive through and eat in the car before heading back home.

The next few days are more exciting, sitting in the office, mainly agreeing to contracts and George and Crater keep recruiting.

One day I manage to get out the office to look at a large empty building, we might buy it and turn it into a hotel.

Then it's time for Grace and Lexie's trip to Snowdon, this time when I take them to school I continue with them to their class.

"My names Jerry." The geography teacher says introducing himself.

"Helena, nice to meet you." I say and shake his hand.

"We are just waiting for the caretaker to check the store room for tents, some of the kids haven't got one."

"Well I brought a few two-man tents, the school can keep them." Crater who's standing behind me places a bag on the table. "Oh, and this is Crater head of my security, there's three black cars that will follow. They won't bother us."

"Yes, the headmaster informed me." He says shaking Craters hand.

I help pack all the gear into the coach, Crater and I take out seats on the coach with Grace and Lexie behind us.

"Any radio chatter?" I ask to the cars behind an hour into the journey.

"Yes, General Helena we heard something about a coach, but then they went radio silent." I hear in my ear piece.

We were told there would be, but I didn't expect it.

We arrive and as I wasn't a part of the planning and even though the geography teacher apparently does it every year, he has messed up. The children have their bags on their backs, but we're left with a pile of tents. I agree to put them in the guard's cars.

"I laugh at the guard's there's about twelve including the two ex SAS all struggling to hide their weapons.

"Look guys," I say to them. "The kids have been told and the local police are aware of our armed presence in the area, you don't have to hide them."

They look relieved to hear this.

I take out my map and take the lead keeping pace with Crater as he uses his cane.

We reach the top a few hours later and stop to eat lunch.

Now it's my turn, I must teach them how to use a map and compass.

I get a bunch of maps and compasses out my bag and hand them out. I tell Grace and Lexie to help their fellow students as they already know how to do it as I taught them both.

A boy and girl who were working together put their hands in the air first, I check their compass bearing and it's correct, so I let them lead the group.

"Helena, we got a problem." I look at the helicopter in the distance, flares begin to pop out the back of it indicating somethings locking on.

"Put the chopper down at the campsite if you can." I say and turn to Crater. "Get one of the snipers to stop here, see if they can spot anything."

Crater nods and goes to give the orders.

When we arrive at the campsite, I spot the helicopter it's sat on a separate field unharmed, both snipers that where on it said they didn't see anything, they could have been hiding in the trees.

The guards now look less menacing as they are helping the kids putting pegs in the ground or showing them how to put up a tent.

Due to someone trying to take down my helicopter, that night I double the guards patrolling the campsite.

40 ENEMY UNKNOWN

I'm woken in the night be shake and a whisper.

"Helena, Ma'am, General Helena."

I climb out the sleeping bag, put on my boots and climb out the tent blinded by a torch.

"What is it?" I ask pushing the torch light out of my eyes.

"We sent a scout out, they've found the enemies camp." That's when I notice it's Crater.

"Are you sure?"

"Yes, they have military weapons and we spotted the surface to air missile, perfect for locking onto helicopters."

"Do we have a few guards we can spare to storm the camp?"

"Yes," he says. "And enough to guard the children."

"Okay, lead the way."

"Kill or capture?" He asks not moving.

It's a serious question, they'd kill me or Grace, maybe even kill Lexie to get at me.

"Kill, capture one." I say it with regret, the less the better. I couldn't forgive myself if we captured them all and if they escaped and hurt Grace, I'd never forgive myself.

We follow the scout, mostly in the dark as we didn't bring night vision.

Eventually we stop, we can see them now as the campfires illuminate several of them.

Crater looks at me for confirmation, "Silencers ready, on your command Crater." I say to him.

We can hear clicking noises as silencers where applied and then they advance, under the advice of Crater we hang back.

From the tree line we watch it unfold, none of the enemy have time to shoot back, it's over before it's begun.

They have one man captured, meaning our time to come out of the tree line.

"You are no General, you and your filthy blood." The captured man says as I approach and spits before one of my soldiers punches him.

"What do you mean filthy blood?" I ask.

"You can't trace your ancestry to an original Templar, like my General can."

"How do you know I can't?" He stays silent. "Crater see what he knows. I'll be in my tent."

"Yes, Ma'am."

I head back to my tent, get back into my sleeping bag, but I can't sleep and eventually I hear the children start to wake, so I decide to get up.

We pack quite slowly, as we are waiting for the coach. When it arrives, I decide to take the helicopter back.

"Ma'am." I hear in my headset.

"What?" I shout over the noise of the helicopter, then I realise the mic at my mouth. "What is it?" I notice the sniper who said it.

"There's a car, fast approaching the coach."

"Can't our cars stop it?"

"No Ma'am. The car is off road approaching side on."

"Pilot, can you pivot so both snipers can get a shot?"

"I can try."

"Sniper will you be able to make the shot?"

"It'll be tricky, but we can try."

"Good fire when ready." I say and wait.

I hear the loud bang, of both weapons over the noise of the helicopter.

"I'm sorry Ma'am we hit the engine block but…"

"But what?" I move and look over his shoulder, all strength drains from me, my hand clutches my locket. "Land the helicopter."

"But Ma'am…"

"Land the helicopter now! That's an order."

"Yes Ma'am."

Before the helicopter can land I jump out and sprint across the field to the overturned coach, the car still stuck inside due to the impact.

"Grace, Lexie, Grace." I call out to the coach but nothing, I hear coughing and spluttering from inside but see no safe way in.

I go to the back where the window is large enough to climb in.

A hand grabs my arm as I go to climb in. I turn and give them a fierce glare; the hand releases and I realise it's Crater.

"Ma'am." He stops. "Helena, the emergency services are coming, you can't get them out without injuring them."

He's right. "Do we have any ex medics? Stretches?"

"One medic and an ex-army surgeon. I think there's four stretches and a few neck braces."

"Then can the surgeon and medic make a safe assessment of how to get them out?"

Crater looks at two of the soldier who nod to him.

"Yes."

"How many stretches can the helicopter hold?"

"Four if only you and the pilot go."

"Then we get Grace and Lexie and two of the severely injured out and get them immediately to hospital."

Crater nods and puts down his cane, the pain instantly visible on his face.

I climb through the back on my hands over broken glass.

I make my way through the mess, I find Lexie who seems to have been thrown from her seat, she squeezes my fingers, but she looks bad. She has several cuts on her face bleeding heavily. I spot Grace in her seat, also looking bad I watch her for a minute and notice her eyes flicker and then I breath in as I was holding my breath hoping she was still breathing.

Then I hear rustling and notice it's the medic, surgeon and Crater.

They put the medic supplies down on the, well on the roof of the coach which has now became the floor.

The two begin to rapidly speak to each other.

It feels like ages, but finally they get Lexie out first as she was easier and closer, she's lying there with a neck brace on, immobilised on a stretcher, she hasn't yet spoke.

They next get Grace out who's in the same state, they load them onto the helicopter.

Two more they pull out of the coach, a boy with his ribs sticking out with serious risk of infection and a girl who broke her thigh bone with serious risk of bleeding to death.

"What's wrong with Grace and Lexie?" I ask while helping load the boy and girl onto the helicopter.

"Internal bleeding maybe, they've got serious bruising on their body, luckily I can't find any broken bones. But they may have head injuries."

I'm even more scared for them, this is all my fault.

"Medic, you should go on the helicopter. You can keep them stable?"

He nods. "I'll do my best Ma'am."

"I can get another passenger." The pilot says looking down at his panel of dials.

"But it won't affect speed?"

"Shouldn't do."

I jump into the passenger seat, while the medics in the back. As we fly away from the scene I spot several ambulances, fire trucks and police cars approaching and a handful of helicopters.

St. Delphine's is the hospital we're going to; I call Lieutenant George who tells me he will be there with soldiers.

41 THE DOCTOR

On arrival I spot the black vehicles, looks like he brought half the security firm.

We land on the helicopter pad, there's doctors and nurses waiting who quickly ferry off the children.

I follow, and a nurse takes me aside trying to stop me, I push past.

"I'm doctor Genethran. Personal doctor for these two girls." A man stated pointing at Lexie and Grace.

"What? No one's told me." The head nurse says.

"A letter from all board members, all managers and all ward managers." He hands it to him, then he begins to read a report the medic gave him, that's when I notice his Templar ring.

I catch him looking at my Templar ring out of the corner of his eye. He must be from the Templar order.

"Are you a relative of any of these children?" Someone asks me.

"Yes, I'm Graces parent and emergency contact for Lexie if you can't reach Roxy and I've been trying but she won't pick up." I start to cry without wanting to, I need to stay strong.

"It's okay, so you know this man, doctor Genethran?"

The man looks at me.

"Yes, I do he's my daughters personal doctor and Lexie's."

The nurse leads me to a waiting area, this time I follow as I'm just in the way.

"Your hands are bleeding." The nurse says, and I totally forgot about them. "We can get them cleaned up."

"No, I'm not going anywhere."

"It's okay, I can do it in here."

I nod, and the nurse comes back with medical supplies and starts picking glass out my hands. The nurse also points at scratches on my neck

175

which I hadn't realised I done.

"I've just been clutching at my locket." I open it and show her.

"She's very beautiful, I think she's lucky to have you."

"I think I'm lucky to have her." I say while the nurse cleans up my chest, then she leaves to dispose of the medical supplies.

The door opens again this time the headmaster appears.

"I'm so sorry." I say. "It's all my fault, Grace and Lexie shouldn't have been on the coach or on that trip the rest of the children would have been safe. I'm sorry."

"I'll have none of that. The police have told me if your soldiers didn't shoot out the engine, there would have been many dead and many severely injured. And you can't stop them two on trips just because they are now shareholders in a multi-million-pound company. You can't stop them having a childhood."

"I know but-" I go to say but he continues.

"I hate cover ups, but we won't say they were after Grace and Lexie, I'll never hear the last of it, ok?"

"Yeah." I say and there's a knock on the door.

"Ma'am." It's George.

"Come in."

"Helena. Thought you'd want to know, they got all the children out no one is dead. Most are being sent here, two are being sent elsewhere, we sent two guards there until their parents arrive."

"Good, has anyone got hold of Roxy yet?"

"No, we sent a soldier. She was at a bunker that must be why her phone doesn't work."

"Inform me if someone reaches her."

"Yes Ma'am."

I still plan on calling her non-stop until she picks up her phone.

The nurse comes back.

"Any news?" I ask.

"Yes, we need you to sign the paperwork for them, they are in surgery both. We are meant to wait for permission, but your doctor wouldn't wait and as we can't get hold of Lexie's mum you'll have to sign her paperwork."

"Yes, fine, that's fine, but are they going to be okay?"

"There is internal bleeding, but they say they'll be okay."

I sit back down, relieved to hear that they will be okay.

"Roxy." I shout when she finally picks up the phone.

"What's wrong? I've got over two hundred missed calls."

"It's Lexie she's in hospital, she's in surgery they say she'll be fine, Grace is in there as well, I'm sorry."

"I'm sure it's not your fault. If she asks for me tell her I love her and that I'll be right, there." I can hear her voice about to go.

I find George, "Send some soldiers to escort Roxy."

"Yes Ma'am."

It feels like hours before the nurse comes back.

"How are they? Are they okay?"

"Yes, they've just came out of surgery. I'll take you to them, they are in the same room against our recommendations, but your doctor wants to keep a close eye on both."

The nurse takes me to a room where both are lying there hooked up to machines, it hurts seeing them like this.

I notice the doctor sitting in the corner reading a magazine.

I take a chair and sit in between them both, holding their hands.

"The Grand Master sent you?" I ask him.

"Yes, when they are fully healed and safe at home he has a mission for you, just you alone, you'll receive more information at the time."

I sit there for a while longer before Roxy comes in, hurrying into the room. We hug and then she looks at Lexie.

"Is she okay?" Roxy asks.

"Yes, she is now, they both had internal bleeding, take my seat." She does. "I'm going to get a drink, you want anything?"

"No, I'm fine thanks."

I head out and George stops me in the corridor.

"Helena, we captured one of the soldiers from the car."

"You've interrogated him?"

"Yes, he says he was acting on orders, what do you want us to do with him?"

"He nearly killed Lexie and Grace, I'll kill him myself, you can keep him until then?"

"Yes Ma'am."

I make my way to the second floor where the shops located.

I'm stopped by a man and woman.

"You saved my daughter." The woman says and throws her arms around me, I feel her wet cheek on my face, from her tear-filled eyes. I hug her back and eventually she releases me.

The man steps in front of me, grips my hand and shakes it. "Thank you." He says and wraps his arm around his wife and leaves with her.

I buy a coffee and head back to the room, taking a seat next to Graces bed.

Grace wakes later that day, it could be night I don't know what time it is. She squeezes my hand.

"What happened? Where am I?" Grace asks in a broken voice.

"You're in hospital." I say, then explain everything.

I feel her warm hand on my face. "I've only ever seen you cry twice." Grace says and wipes away a tear.

"Yes, and both times I've been worried about you." I say and rest my head on her, I can't hug her I nearly accidently strangled her last time.

We talk for a while longer, Lexie also awake now. They decide to sleep which means I can go take care of business.

I take a car with soldiers to a barn where Crater is holding the man.

My boots click as I walk on the wooden panels the soldiers part as I make my way through the barn, that's when I notice Crater standing before the prisoner.

"He said much?" I ask holding out my palm outstretched.

"No, there was a second guy that ran but he won't say where." Crater says and puts a gun in my hand.

"Where's your friend?" I ask pointing the gun at him. "Where's your General?" Nothing, I pull the trigger. He wasn't going to say anything. "Clean it up please, return back to normal duties and send a small team to try find the other guy."

Crater nods, I give back the gun and head back to the hospital.

Grace and Lexie seem better, both eating the doctor folds his paper and stands.

"I've checked them both and after major surgery they seem to be in good health. I'd say they can go home tomorrow. Lots of rest and no school until the stiches come out."

"How long will that be?" I ask.

"Two weeks, minimum." He says. "Can we talk outside?"

"I can't thank you enough for saving them." I say to him when we get outside.

He waves his hand to say it's nothing but adds: "It's no problem." He says and hands me a piece of paper. "I'll expect they should be roughly better in two weeks, on the fourth week the Grand Master expects you to meet an agent, alone to get a somewhat better understanding of the Order. Call the number on the back and you'll receive a location." He shakes my hand and walks off down the corridor.

42 MYSTERIOUS AGENT

The first week we let Megan manage the company the second week we decide it's unfair, so we take turns in minding them both.

The middle of the third week they get their stiches out and seem fine enough for school but no exercise for a week.

Fourth week comes, and I must call the number, when I do an agent tells me to meet him outside a train station in town.

"I'll be gone two days max, Roxy and Lexie are coming here."

"But why?" Grace asks. "I can go to Roxy's."

"Because, it's easier to secure here."

"Ok." She says and hugs me tightly.

I hug her several more times before eventually leaving.

As I do Roxy arrives with Lexie, she still refuses to buy a car as her so called husband has it, but she still hasn't seen him yet. So, her guards drive her about.

We talk a little, but now I'm running late, I take the train as I'm not allowed my car.

It's a short walk through the city, past the hustle and bustle. Sometimes I miss the quiet especially when shopping now I must take some several armed guards.

But mainly I like my life now, I just wish someone wasn't trying to kill me.

I spot the agent smoking a cigarette under a street light, he flicks it into the street as he spots me approaching.

"Hello, I'm Helena and you are?"

"I'm the agent." He says with a grin.

Well I knew that.

"Yes, but your name?" I ask.

"Oh, a name, just call me agent."

"But why won't you give me a name?"

"Because, I'm an agent. Come on my cars around the corner."

We get to his car, he drives a short distance and parks up over the road from an apartment block.

"What are we doing here?"

"Waiting." He says with a grin.

"Ok. Then what is it you do?"

"Anything a General wants as long as the Grand Master agrees."

"So, I can command you?" I ask.

"No, not yet. I'm here to show you what we do, what sort of missions you'll send your soldiers on."

We sit in silence until a black van screeches to a halt outside the apartment block. Then a woman comes out dragging another woman and throws them into the back of the van, then the woman jumps into the passenger seat.

I go to grab my gun, but the agent grabs my wrist.

"Not yet." He says starting the engine and begins to follow the black van.

It heads into the countryside and stops at a gate which leads to a dirt road through a wooded area.

But we must drive past so that they don't get suspicious.

We drive for a little while before finding somewhere appropriate to park.

The agent climbs a wall, I follow. We are in a forest.

Something about a forest makes me feel calm, the sound of the wind brushing through the leaves and the crunching of branches and twigs underfoot.

"Do you know where we are going?" I ask after walking for what feels like longer than it should have been. We should have at least saw the van by now.

"Yes, the road zig zags. I thought their operation was here, but I had to be sure."

"Doing what? What are they…" I stop as he suddenly stops. His face seems to lose all colour.

Then I notice it, a wire pressing into the fabric of his shin.

He lets out a sigh, "Listen carefully, find where the wire goes, it should be a bomb."

I follow the wire carefully to a bomb.

"Now what?"

"Now, listen even more carefully."

He explains and talks me through how to defuse it, I double check everything he tells me to do.

"Now what?" I ask again as he has just stopped giving me instructions.

"Find the biggest tree and hide. If I've given you the wrong instructions, then there's no point in us both dying."

I find a tree and wait, there's no noise then laughter, when I come out from behind the tree he's walking in circles.

"I guess we go on more slowly." I say, and he nods and sits down.

"Before we get to their lodge, whatever you see in there just try not to let it get to you."

"I don't scare easily." I say and drink some water.

"Guns out then." He says standing up.

I secure my bag tightening the straps across my chest and waist, then pull out both guns.

We start to walk up a small hill, once at the top I spot the van first then the lodge.

"There doesn't seem to be any movement inside." I say.

"Come on."

I look through a window, finding no one.

The agent opens the door, I follow. The place looks too clean. No dishes, nothing out of place.

The agent goes straight to the bedroom as if he knows where he's going. He grabs the end of the bed and gently begins to lift it.

I watch as the bed continues to rise, revealing stairs that lead downwards. We begin our descent.

There's a corridor with many rooms, I go into the first one. The agent shines a torch, there's blood everywhere as if someone had attempted to mop it up but then decided against it as there's too much.

When we step back into the corridor there's a light coming from one of the rooms.

We quietly make our way to the room while attaching our silencers.

I peek around the corner it's the woman who was dragging the other woman. She's sitting at a desk.

I step inside, she quickly stands up and goes to shoot, I shoot first and catch her body before it hits the floor.

There's not much in here only a laptop. We move on.

We push through a sort of flap into a large room, cold, very cold.

In the centre the kidnapped woman is lying on a slab, one of them surgeon lights above her, illuminating her.

I notice a bone saw flying through the air, I just barely act in time to see it fly past my face.

The agent can't get a clear shot and I've dropped one of my guns.

I manage to shoot him in the knee before he knocks the other gun out my hand.

But I also knock the bone saw out of his hand, I can hear the muffled screams of the woman on the table and I can now smell bleach.

He isn't a fighter, I punch him in the face then quickly in the throat before finally kicking him in the stomach.

He stumbles backwards, and I drop to the floor, the agent taps twice two bullets to the head.

I get to the table and begin to undo the straps and remove a rag in the woman's mouth.

She gets to her feet and grabs a scalpel.

"It's okay," I say. "We're…" What are we.

"Part of a task force, she's got a badge, I don't." The agent says.

I fumble in my jacket and throw it to her in panic, the last thing I want is her attempting to attack me.

She picks it up, looks at the picture and begins to look back and forth at me, just to confirm that it is me.

"It says you're from an order."

"Yes, to tackle unlicensed procedures like this surgeon performs." I lie.

She throws it back and puts down the scalpel and begins to shiver.

I put my jacket over her and lead her outside.

We wait for a clean-up crew from the Templar order. They arrive, and the woman goes into the back of a black ambulance.

"What will happen to her?" I ask the agent.

"Sent home, sworn to secrecy and a sum of money to help her keep quiet."

"But who were they?"

"Well he was a surgeon, his wife as well probably. I thought that was obvious."

"So why the cloak and dagger? Why not just call the police?"

"You saw the bloodied floor that was one room and you saw that there were several doorways. They've probably killed hundreds conducting all sorts of crazy medical procedures." He pauses. "If we called the police they would have just ran and continued to do it underground, it's already hard to find them."

"There's more crazy surgeons then?"

"Not just surgeons, scientists, cults. Doing things that would keep the world awake at night."

"And it's my job to send soldiers to deal with these people?" I ask still somewhat confused that I'm here.

He opens his mouth then quickly shuts it. "That's not my place to say."

"Yes, yes, it's the Grand Masters place to tell me, any advice for me?"

"You haven't had a call from him yet?" I shake my head. "Then when you do panic, he hardly ever makes a phone call." He picks his bag up. "That car," he says pointing, "will drop you off at home, I am off to Egypt."

"Good luck." I say and shake his hand.

The car drops me off at home, on the way there the driver stays silent and doesn't even answer me, but he did know where I live.

I get changed into comfier clothes and get comfy on the couch with Grace, we decide to do a movie marathon and have a lazy day.

43 PARTY

The next few weeks and months the company continues to make large profits and continues to grow. I have many soldiers now, but all has been silent from the Grand Master.

Not even any strange missions or agent.

We decide to celebrate the company's success by holding a party in one of the large conference rooms of the building that we just acquired to turn into a hotel.

Everyone agrees that family should be allowed, so we arrange it in time for when Grace and Lexie have a week off for half term.

On the day of the party I'm quite busy I have things to arrange like food and security. Anyone that's single or doesn't have family said they are happy to work, luckily there's enough of them so I don't have to hire extra.

Then once everything is done I head back home to get changed and pick Grace up.

Grace is still doing her hair by the time I'm ready to go.

"Just because you have super speed when it comes to getting ready." She says to me as I take the hair brush from her to help.

"I don't have super speed, I just manage my time." I say brushing her hair.

"How?" She looks at me in the mirror mid putting on her shoe. "You're the only girl I know who can get ready super-fast."

I shrug my shoulders and continue brushing.

"I guess I got skills." I say.

She helps zip my dress up. I'm wearing the white one she got me for my birthday.

Graces phone which is on the table begins to ring.

"It's Lexie, probably wondering where we are." Grace says answering the phone.

"Tell her I'm coming to pick them up. You are ready now?"

"Yep." She says and stands up picking up her bag and begins to talk on the phone.

I've got two cars following me for security, I pick up Roxy and Lexie. Another two security cars follow.

We all look smart, we take a picture under Graces request and eventually all agree on a picture where we are all are not blinking or sneezing.

Megan's waiting for us outside looking frozen, there's many soldiers with guns and our new dog unit.

I give Megan my jacket and link arms then we walk up the steps together.

"Thanks," she says. "Everyone's waiting inside."

They start clapping as we enter the room, which I don't get. Are they clapping because we look good I mean we do but I doubt they are doing it for that. It's an odd social thing I may one day understand.

We make our way to the stage, I got out of making a speech as I'm quite bad at them.

Megan and Roxy are doing the speech together, they talk of the company's success and thank everyone. They also make a joke about if they wander around the rest of the building they'll need to wear a hard hat. I find it funny with everyone else but it's kind of not a joke they would need a hard hat as it's still a building site.

After the speech I go around the room meeting new people, their wives, husbands, sons, daughters. It does feel like I'm building something good, a community even if some of the business requires killing.

Seeing many faces makes me dizzy or that could be the alcohol, either way I'm glad when my phone goes so that I can excuse myself.

But before I can excuse myself guards rush the stage and begin to follow the exit protocol ushering us out the back.

"What's going on?" I ask as more guards flood in front and behind us, loading their weapons.

"Convoy just turned up out the front, your house is also compromised. They haven't engaged yet, but they are not friendly, Roxy house has also been hit."

"What about the guests?"

"They are going out through the basement like we planned. Which links up to the car park. Once the guests are gone we will flank them from the car park."

My phone still ringing, someone is trying really hard to get hold of me. I search for, Grace, Lexie, Roxy and Megan once I know they are with us I answer the phone in case they know who's the convoy out front is.

There's no caller ID, but this also must not be a coincidence it must be important.

"Hello, it's Helena."

"Yes, I know," the voice is deep but slow and calculated, "I need you to come to the headquarters. This is the Grand Master." I panic.

Great headquarters doesn't sound good.

Printed in Great Britain
by Amazon